You Call That Service?

©Hiroki Ozaki

CONTENTS

©Hiroki Ozaki

"Starting today, I, Shiren Fuyukura, am your master! Serve me well!"

Shiren Fuyukura

©Hiroki Ozaki

Alfoncina XIII

Sasara Tatsunami

Kiyomizu Jouryuuji

Tamaki Shijou

©Hiroki Ozaki

©Hiroki Ozaki

KISETSU MORITA

Illustration by
HIROKI OZAKI

You Call That Service?, Vol. 1

Kisetsu Morita

Translation by Jasmine Bernhardt
Cover art by Hiroki Ozaki

OMAE NO GOHOSHI WA SONO TEIDOKA? volume 1
Copyright © 2011 Kisetsu Morita
Illustrations copyright © 2011 Hiroki Ozaki
All rights reserved.
Original Japanese edition published in 2011 by SB Creative Corp.

This English edition is published by arrangement with SB Creative Corp., Tokyo in care of Tuttle-Mori Agency, Inc., Tokyo.

English translation © 2019 by Yen Press, LLC

Yen On
150 West 30th Street, 19th Floor
New York, NY 10001

Visit us at yenpress.com
facebook.com/yenpress
twitter.com/yenpress
yenpress.tumblr.com
instagram.com/yenpress

First Yen On Edition: December 2019

Yen On is an imprint of Yen Press, LLC.
The Yen On name and logo are trademarks of Yen Press, LLC.

Library of Congress Cataloging-in-Publication Data
Names: Morita, Kisetsu, author. | Ozaki, Hiroki, illustrator. | Bernhardt, Jasmine, translator.
Title: You call that service? / Kisetsu Morita ; illustration by Hiroki Ozaki ; translation by Jasmine
    Bernhardt ; cover art by Hiroki Ozaki.
Other titles: Omae no gohoshi wa sono teidoka?. English
Description: First Yen On edition. | New York, NY : Yen On, 2019–
Identifiers: LCCN 2019036814 | ISBN 9781975305628 (v. 1 ; trade paperback)
Subjects: CYAC: Vampires—Fiction. | Love—Fiction. | Humorous stories.
Classification: LCC PZ7.1.M6725 Yo 2019 | DDC [Fic]—dc23
LC record available at https://lccn.loc.gov/2019036814

ISBNs: 978-1-9753-0562-8 (paperback)
        978-1-9753-0563-5 (ebook)

10 9 8 7 6 5 4 3 2 1

LSC-C

Printed in the United States of America

©Hiroki Ozaki

PROLOGUE

"Hey, Ryouta, it's morning already. Seven twenty-five. You'll be late!"

Rustle, rustle. A large shudder shook Ryouta's bed.

"I can't; I'm sleepy…"

Ryouta was usually the one doing the waking up, but making lunch the night before had taken longer than he expected and kept him up late.

He could barely open his eyes, mostly because he wasn't used to being woken up. He'd been having a rather lovely dream, too, so his instincts were screaming, *I don't want to get up!*

"Up, up, up! I need my traditional breakfast of rice and miso soup and eggs and fried fish! It will take longer for us to get to school now that we've moved!"

The force that shook him grew stronger. *Rustle, rustle, rustle.*

"Nnngh… This train's a shaky one…"

"Ryouta, this is not your master's job; it's yours! You're supposed to say, *Get up; it's morning. Sheesh, Master, you lazy piece of work— But out of respect for your childlike sleeping face, I suppose I'll allow another five minutes!* You need to be more conscious of what kind of minion you—"

"Hey, Ouka, don't sleep in the family altar. I know you like high places, but you're in the way! I can see up your skirt, Ouka!"

The girl snapped when she heard that name.

After all, it wasn't hers.

"If you do not wake up in the next three seconds, I'll **bite** you. This is a real three-second rule."

Bite. When he heard that word, Ryouta's consciousness rapidly tried to awaken.

Things were headed south!

But three seconds were still plenty of time. No need to panic.

"Three... Two..."

Chomp.

"O-owwwwwwwwwwwwwwwwwwwwwwwwww!!"

Pain coursed through his neck, and Ryouta leaped up. Wasn't there still one second left?!

The girl had clamped down on the base of his neck so hard her teeth pierced his skin.

"Oh, you're *ahake*. I *has* gonna *hite* you *hecause* you weren't."

"Don't talk while you're biting me! Don't bite me, period!" he yelled, and the girl finally let him go.

Her long hair, tied in pigtails, swayed side to side more violently than usual. The exaggerated action was a sign she was angry.

Even her smallish and fairly cute face had a tinge of red to it.

Her face is red almost all the time anyway because she gets mad so quickly, though, Ryouta thought. But he only thought it. He'd be given a blood punishment if he said it out loud.

A literal blood punishment...

"You were not waking up at all, so I bit you. Ryouta, it seems you've forgotten you are a minion in service of me—of Shiren Fuyukura. And that's your punishment."

"You just bit me before the three seconds were up! I got up with godlike speed!"

"Hmph. Bloodsucking is a typical form of intimate contact between Sacred Blooded masters and their minions. Be grateful I'm even going out of my way to warn you. Thank me as a good Christian would pledge devotion to the Virgin Mary."

"You're a god now?"

"Of course, you may return home to Japan from the **Empire**. There's a ninety-nine percent chance you'll be caught along the way, though."

"Crap... She's sizing me up..."

The bell on Ryouta's neck rang when he stood.

There was a **collar** around his neck. When they went to and from school, he would be dragged along by a chain.

That pretty much summed up his situation. He had no choice but to live his life as the property of this high school girl named Shiren Fuyukura.

If he walked around without his collar on, then the good people of the town would turn rabid and attack him.

"All right, I'm making breakfast. I've still got time." Ryouta slowly stood from his bed, but just before he reached the door, Shiren clung to him from behind.

It wasn't a romantic gesture; she was seizing him more than anything.

She was so small, she was almost like a little sister coming up to play with him.

"Hey, I take back what I said before… Pretend I never said you could go back to Japan. Don't go back, even if there's only a one percent chance you'd be caught…"

Her nails dug into his hips.

At least cut your nails if you're going to cling to me like this.

Shiren Fuyukura was much too terrified of being left alone.

Sheesh, she always looks down her nose at me and pushes me around, and now this.

He wanted to tell her to grow up, but…well, it wouldn't hurt to stay awhile. A promise was a promise.

"Without you, I'd…I'd…"

"I know. I'm not going back. Don't worry."

"Really…? It's a thousand needles for you if you lie to your master!"

"Yeah, yeah, I know."

"And a blood donation penalty of fifteen hundred milliliters!"

"Yeah, that's not that— Wait, I'd die! That's almost enough to kill a grown man! That's three times more than a typical donation!"

"Hmm. Two thousand, then."

"You're not even hiding that you're trying to kill me… You are, aren't you?!"

"You oblivious baboon! My point is that you're not supposed to leave!

Be more conscious of your master's feelings! You still lack heart in your service, Ryouta!"

Shiren clung to him harder.

It wasn't so bad to be depended on like this, was it? Shiren was kind of cute, too...

"I'm telling you, it's oka—"

"Without you, I'd have to be the one to clean and cook and do laundry and weed the garden and swap out my residence permit at city hall! I hate how much work it is! You're the one who's supposed to do all that, and I'm the one who supports you!"

"...So that's the punch line we're going with?" Ryouta sighed, regretting all the unnecessary things he'd done in the past.

If only he hadn't gone hiking that day...

Ryouta was living together with (well, more like living rent-free with) a girl of Sacred Blood—what we'd call a vampire. He had reached the neighboring village and discovered it was a country of vampires called the Sacred Blood Empire, and he couldn't go back to Japan.

As of now, it didn't seem like he'd be going back any time soon.

©Hiroki Ozaki

Ryouta
Asagiri

This is my very first minion, who wandered in from Japan.

EPISODE 1
LET'S GO TO THE SACRED BLOOD EMPIRE!

Ryouta Asagiri never watched the news.

In terms of current events, he really only knew the prime minister's name. Well, maybe—he wasn't completely sure.

He was in his second year of high school, and his favorite thing to do, bar none, was hiking far away from people.

"The mountain's not that tall, but the slope's pretty steep…," Ryouta Asagiri muttered to himself on the empty mountain. It was a lonely hobby, but that was the goal.

The moment he stepped onto the path that led up the ridgeline, his cell phone started buzzing.

"Let me guess… Yep. Knew it…"

TITLE: To Ryouta
MESSAGE: Dearest Ryouta, where are you? I am so rather worried because I don't know where you are. Because I'm your… Oh! Don't make me say any more! Tomorrow's Monday, isn't it? I will make lunch for you with the utmost skill and the care of a loving wife. As the secret ingredient, I will use my bodil a spice that is not sold any-where in the world. Then I believe you'll be mine. I had wonderful dreams last night because I fell asleep with my recording of your voice on repeat. Thank you.
Yours truly, Kiyomizu Jouryuuji

It looked as if she was going to write *bodily fluids*, but maybe that was just his imagination.

"I still have service out here? Phones these days are nuts…"

This wasn't a threatening message, just a text from a classmate, but sometimes those messages wore away at his soul as effectively as a threat would anyway.

He was already fed up with that one, and another one came.

TITLE: Sorry!!!
MESSAGE: You left this morning because you're mad at what I did, right? I'm so sorry!!! It's important to remember your manners, even with close relatives! I mean, I get it; anyone would get mad if someone tried to take their underwear off while they were sleeping. But I didn't mean anything weird, okay? I just remembered I had to do laundry, and that's why I was trying to take them off you. I don't feel guilty about it at all. It's not like...I can't look at you as my little brother anymore. It's not like...I can't handle it. I can't stand it anymore; just thinking of you makes me hot, Ryo... It's not like that at all! This is a misunderstanding! It's nothing! I don't love you like THAT! That could never happen! Not in a million years!
Rei Asagiri

"Oh. Just my sister."

It was from a relative with the same last name.

"I think I should just throw my phone away..."

Ryouta liked his casual hiking. The empty mountainous wilderness was the only place he could find peace.

To put it simply, Ryouta was so attractive that it put his life in danger.

He knew exactly why that was. Three out of every five people who met his grandfather didn't recognize the man as human. Of course, that brought up an interesting philosophical question of whether he was really human if more than half of his own kind didn't recognize him as such, but we'll skip over that.

In his day, it was typical for families to go to matchmakers, but his grandfather was single for a very long time. He only managed to get married just before he turned fifty, and that was with a woman who had an obsession with strange animals, among other odd interests.

His grandfather regretted his life, so he hid in the mountains and carried out some esoteric ritual. According to some reports, his request was something along the lines of *In exchange for the last thirty years of my life, my grandson will lead a life attractive to women when he is of age!*

And that was extremely effective on Ryouta.

His grandfather, by the way, was still alive at ninety-eight years old. And that was after he'd lost thirty years of his life, supposedly. Maybe he wasn't human after all.

"This is bad. Kiyomizu's text brought up some dark memories…"

For example, on Valentine's Day in his first year of high school, Ryouta received a total of more than five hundred chocolates. There were only four hundred girls in his high school.

You jealous? Go ahead—take my place.

Because if this keeps up, I'm not gonna live long, you know.

First, he'd been attacked by jealous guys. He remembered feeling his face go pale when both the karate and judo clubs ganged up on him at the same time.

There were times when the girls chased him like stalkers, as with Kiyomizu's text.

"Rei, just give me a break… I somehow managed to get out by saying I was off hiking. If I stayed in the house any longer…"

A genuine shiver passed through Ryouta when he remembered what had happened that morning. If he had been just a second too late, he really would've been stripped.

"And my sister's not the only one. Kiyomizu's been getting worse and worse, too…"

Kiyomizu Jouryuuji was the only daughter of a family that owned a temple, and Ryouta's classmate.

She was rather rich, so she often had bronze statues of Ryouta installed around school. Just last week, the number of Ryoutas rose to thirty-eight, more than all the statues of past principals combined.

Not only that, but it seemed as if she had been more active recently. The other day, he'd found a letter from her in their postbox that said "I'm always watching, <3" along with a photo of him in the bath.

Once he started thinking about how she could have managed to take the picture, it would be all over for him.

To make matters worse, Kiyomizu was beautiful enough that there was a secret society of dubious origin called "Protectors of Kiyomizu and Her Small Tits," and their members would come after him, too.

"I mean, I'm glad I'm attractive, okay? But I might end up dead one of these days because of it... And I haven't even found where my first crush has gone yet, either..."

Because of his somber mood, the hike took longer than he planned, but he finally made it off the mountain and into the city of Akinomiya.

This time, he'd taken the five-hour trail that went from the city Ryouta lived in, Oshiro, to the neighboring city. Akinomiya was a rural city in the valley with a population of roughly thirty thousand. The freeway cut straight through the mountain, and a local train line that headed to the Sanin Region in the west came by every twenty minutes.

It was a lesser-known path, so there weren't any other climbers, but he noticed the Self-Defense Force was roaming around the entrance to the mountain.

"I wonder if there was an accident. There weren't any landslides or anything."

But—

"It's awfully quiet for being back in civilization."

—even after coming down the hill and entering the residential area, it was eerily empty. After five minutes of walking, still not a single car had passed by.

"I wish there were a few more people around..."

Finally, he saw a passerby approaching him.

But it wasn't the kind of person he was hoping for—it was a girl around middle school age.

Her blonde hair was tied back into two pigtails. Even Ryouta, who had had more than enough of girls, found his heart skipping a beat at her beautiful face. She was perfectly balanced on the line between cute and beautiful.

Man, she's cute... No, wait, girls are my enemy...

He had a bad feeling about this. It would only spell trouble for him if she suddenly told him she had fallen in love at first sight.

Of course, it wasn't as if every woman he met fell in love with him upon seeing him; he was just being excessively self-conscious.

Easy, Ryouta, calm down. He just needed to keep a straight face and walk right past her. Just keep a straight face.

She was getting closer and closer.

Easy, calm down.

"Um, excuse me!" But the girl suddenly stepped right in Ryouta's path.

Uh-oh, I feel a confession coming on… This just happened last week… She was a middle school girl, too, and when I turned her down, she started crying. She wouldn't stop, and for some reason, it ended up being my fault.

But he didn't yet know for sure that she was going to do the same thing.

"Y-yeah…? What do you need…?"

"Erm, are you…Japanese?"

That was a weird question, but the girl seemed very serious. Her lips were even quivering. Maybe she lost a bet?

"Yeah. My parents, my grandmother, and my grandfather—well, probably—are all Japanese."

"Is that so? Excellent! I am so glad to hear it! I feel like I've encountered a yeti or a snake cryptid in the mountains!"

That was an oddly rude comparison. Ryouta wasn't a cryptid.

He was starting to get a little nervous.

"Erm, what was I supposed to ask next…? Um…?"

The girl, still standing in front of him, opened a book to check something. The book was called *My First Minion.* Her first *what?* He sure hoped he misread that.

"Um, do you have any urgent business? Do you have any sick relatives you must go see right away? A lover who's being transferred overseas whom you have to see off tonight? Or must you return quickly to a tyrant lest your friend Selinuntius be executed? Do you need to defeat a monster in the next three minutes in order to stay on this planet?"

"I don't have any sick parents or any kind of lover, I'm not the main character of *Run, Melos,* and I'm not from Nebula M78, so I'm good."

Maybe this girl was the one who wasn't Japanese, and she was practicing to see if her language skills were good enough for conversation. She had blonde hair anyway. But her Japanese was flawless.

The girl looked back down to her book.

©Hiroki Ozaki

"I see. Then what do you think of Japan's system of lifetime employment? If you could work, bound to a wonderful company until retirement age, would you choose that over an occupation with an uncertain future?"

"Huh? Is this a street survey? Sure, I guess downsizing and relying on temp work sounds like it could create some problems, and I don't want my parents to worry, so I guess I'd prefer a stable job."

The girl's excitement seemed to be growing with every question he answered, until it was nearly spilling over.

"Then this is my last request. Please pose as though you've found ten thousand yen by your feet and are going to pick it up."

Of course, that was when he got a bad feeling about this.

"I'm sorry if this is a creepy thing to say, but I'm going to say it anyway: Don't kiss me while I'm bending down, okay?"

The girl froze. A tremble traveled through her face.

"One time, an elementary school girl told me the same thing, and she almost kissed me... I don't know why you were asking me those questions, but just in case..."

"I-it's all right! I'm not going to kiss you! I've made my promise to the Emperor!"

"Emperor? What emperor? Well, whatever. I'm getting down now. There."

Then the girl approached slowly. "Stay still."

"Uh, sure, but what are you going to do?" He really had no idea what she wanted.

"I am going to bite you."

In the next moment, an intense pain coursed through the base of his neck.

"OWWWWWWWWWWWWWWWWWWW!!"

It hurt enough that he could tell—she really and truly bit him!

"Is this that curse again?! I've been attacked by a girl who wouldn't let go until she got her kiss, but not by a girl who's into biting!"

The sharp pain quickly subsided. The girl, however, still hadn't let go. She also had a grip on his arms, probably to keep him from running away.

"*Yesh*, I did it. *Ah* long *ah* I go *hlow*, I can do it '*he hirs* time… It said so in '*he tek'guk*."

The girl sounded nervous. She would sometimes murmur to herself as her teeth still dug into him.

She seemed so earnest, he almost wanted to cheer her on— *No, wait, hold on! She's still biting me, in the present progressive tense! I'm losing blood!*

But he didn't feel any pain. He almost even felt nice.

And he was too relaxed to run away. He couldn't build the strength to do anything.

He wasn't sure how long her teeth were sunk into him, but when she finally let go, he was practically unconscious.

"Boy, what's your name?"

She was no longer acting like a nervous kitten. She'd played him…

"Ry… Ryouta Asagiri…," he answered, his mind still fuzzy.

He couldn't work up the will to disobey her, almost as though he was hypnotized.

"And how old are you? What year are you in?"

"H… High school, second year…"

"Well! That's the same as me. Yes, very good, very good. What a good boy." The girl wore a big smile on her face; he wouldn't be surprised if she struck a pose right then.

"We're in the same year? But you look like a…middle school kid…," Ryouta questioned, everything in his mind still feeling distant. His voice felt as if it would fail him soon, too.

"I do not! How could I look like anything but a high schooler?! According to both Japan's and the Empire's laws, I am a high school student!"

Her irritated tone forcibly pulled his fading consciousness back.

"Very well, Ryouta. Starting today, you are a minion belonging to me, Shiren Fuyukura. That means you are my kin, my retainer, my help, and my butler all in one. You will serve me well! I may even grant you a bonus depending on your performance!"

Minion? That wasn't a word he heard all that often. He wasn't sure if being a butler or a maid counted as being a minion, though.

"Then, Ryouta, here is your first order."

He was about to pass out for real this time. The girl's voice was faint and distant now.

"You shall never leave me alone."

That was an oddly pessimistic order, and kinda clingy.

Ryouta's consciousness then completely vanished, leaving him to his dreams.

Dreams typically come in two kinds: dreams the dreamer knows are dreams, and the ones they don't.

That's why Ryouta figured this must have been the former.

He was in his fourth-grade classroom, feeling nervous and restless because all the girls in the class were staring at him. That had been hard on little Ryouta.

"Asagiri is so cool, isn't he?"

"He's not immature like the other boys."

"I'm going to give him chocolate on Valentine's Day because I *really* love him!"

He would pretend he never heard any of that gossip. It was all because of the spell anyway, not because he was actually good-looking. He didn't want to be this attractive; he just wanted to be regular friends with girls.

But there was just one girl who showed no interest in him.

"Come on, you shouldn't bother Ryouta like that," she cautioned the others with an annoyed look. "At this rate, he won't be able to come to school anymore because of the stress, and then you'll just be upset. Think a little bit about the future."

And with that, the other girls stopped gossiping.

Ouka Sarano—whenever she entered the classroom, the eyes focused on Ryouta found something else to look at.

She had bright, un-Japanese-like red hair and clear blue eyes. Her face was also intimidatingly beautiful, keeping others at a safe distance from her, and she was like the queen of the class.

She was also the only girl among them who wasn't captivated by Ryouta.

"Thanks, Ouka, as always."

"I'm not asking favors from you for this, so don't worry. But you're responsible, too. You're too indecisive, Ryouta. You're going to make a lot of girls cry when you grow up. You need to fix this lifestyle of yours before you get yourself killed."

"*Killed?* That's too much."

"Slaughtered, then."

"Okay, but that synonym still means the same thing!"

"Kids frolic around
In the frozen Siberian plain
Like arctic hares
Licking the snow."

"Why did you turn it into poetry?! That's some weird imagery you have going on there!"

"Then how about this?
Kites fly energetically
In the sky like birds
Little kids swim around
Like fish in school swimsuits."

"Okay, whatever. But please don't talk about little kids like that."

Ouka was always like this; her outspoken nature was just the beginning.

But her frankness on the topic made Ryouta happy. Ouka was the only one in his class who looked at him not as a boy, but as a classmate.

That was why it wouldn't be out of the question for him to develop a crush on her.

She was the only one he could fall in love with, one-on-one as humans.

"But, yeah, I guess if in seven years you find yourself in a mess you can't get out of, come to me." She stood before him, then poked him on the forehead with her nail. "Then I'll protect you from all the bothers of the world."

She smiled like a queen. She kinda was; she was rich enough to be picked up and dropped off at school in a car with tinted windows.

"R-really…?"

"Yes. The Emperor's word, once passed, never returns. A ruler never goes back on her word."

It was almost like a proposal, so Ryouta found himself flustered and stuck. "Ah, ah, ah, ahhhhhhh…"

"And in return, you can expect to lose some parts if you get into any strange relationships."

"I'm losing what?! That's terrifying!"

"Here's a hint: You can sell it on the black market."

"This is getting graphic! Stop!"

—But despite everything, Ouka Sarano transferred to another school the next day without a single word.

It was so sudden, not even the school could figure out where she transferred to.

Still, ever since that day, Ouka remained Ryouta's first crush.

Couldn't Ouka come save him from this random act of violence?

Ryouta knew he would have collapsed after losing so much blood from his neck, which was why he knew this was also a dream.

Was he about to die…?

The dream wasn't in his elementary school anymore. The background was just a cheap, blank canvas.

But then—

"You're stupid, Ryouta. I said I was going to protect you, so I am. Rulers keep their word. That is a truth as unshakable as an oracle from heaven itself."

—Ouka appeared before him.

"Now, take my hand. I'll lead the way!"

"Ouka… Huh?"

When Ryouta reached out, he woke up. He had been sleeping in an unfamiliar bed.

"No, is someone…?"

He immediately checked beside him. It wouldn't be entirely unthinkable to find a naked girl sleeping next to him. His sister had just assaulted him that morning.

No one was in the bed but him. He was safe.

"Then who saved me? Wait, that girl could have had an accomplice…"

When he checked his phone, he found 136 unread texts from Kiyomizu. He deleted them all.

"First I need to look around to see if anyone's— What the heck is this?!"

Just as he noticed the unfamiliar weight on his neck, he heard something ringing. When he looked in the mirror in the room, he saw on his neck a collar with a bell.

"A collar?! I haven't been kidnapped, have I?! Am I in a pervert's house?!"

Nervous, Ryouta checked the room. If this place belonged to some unhinged stranger, he had to get out of there right away! There wasn't any chain attached to the collar, so he could escape.

The room was dull, nothing particularly distinctive about it. At most, there was a calendar on the wall. Today was September 8, Monday. Hopefully, there wasn't anything like "BITE" written on the day…

8ᴛʜ DAY IN THE MONTH OF REVOLUTION
TAIAN GOODBLOOD

"Huh…? What's the Month of Revolution? Is this some new zodiac thing?"

Ryouta flipped through several pages of the calendar. All the names of the months he found gave him some pause, like the Month of Development, Month of Great Victory, Month of the Empire, and on and on.

Just as Ryouta was wondering if it belonged to a girl obsessed with horoscopes, he heard a voice coming from behind him.

"Oh, you've awakened. How have your first moments as a minion been? Starting today, I, Shiren Fuyukura, am your master! Serve me well!"

There was no doubt about it—this girl was the one who had bitten his neck.

She made a grand sweeping motion to place her hand on her chest. It didn't seem as if she was planning on including an apology in the first thing she said to him, and that got under his skin a little.

"Fuyukura, right? You really shouldn't go up to people and just bite—"

"Now, my minion, here is your first job: Clean this room!" Shiren pointed straight at Ryouta.

"Hey, don't point at people. It's rude."

"Listen. Be sure to separate the plastic and paper garbage. Plastic bags go with the plastic. Wait, how do you dispose of spray cans? Oh, and there is some kind of cockroach antenna on the floor in the corner, so get rid of it as quickly as possible."

"Come on, quit pointing…"

"The vacuum is one of those newer models that can get into every nook and cranny. It's in the back of that closet there. Open the windows when you use it to get the dust out and the fresh air in."

"Stop pointing at me! It's really getting on my nerves!"

"This will be your bedroom from now on, Ryouta. But you may not hide any naughty books beneath your bed— Hey, you need to get cleaning!"

"Then, put your finger down! And I'm asking you to explain what's going on!"

"Please clean for me."

"No, not even if you ask nicely."

"Please, cleaning, *s'il vous plait*, okay?"

"Not even if you use French. And I'm pretty sure you just said *please* twice."

The girl's expression quickly clouded over. "Hey, why isn't my minion listening to my orders…? Then cook for me. I want bright-red omelet and rice today. You will write your master's name—Shiren—on the egg with ketchup. The kanji characters are *shi* as in 'poetry,' and *ren* as in 'compassion.'"

"Nope. That's too much to write with ketchup."

"…Then weed the yard. The backyard is infested. I cannot stand those bloodsucking mosquitoes. The only one allowed to suck blood around here is me, you see."

"Do it yourself. You order me around anymore, and I'm spraying some bug repellent in that mouth of yours."

"I'm telling you to do *something*! Fulfill your duty as my minion!"

"I still don't get what you mean by *minion*! You came out of nowhere and bit me—who do you think you are?!"

"No… He didn't turn into my minion?"

The girl (apparently named Shiren) pulled out the strange book titled *My First Minion* and started flipping through the pages. It was the same one she'd had when they first met.

She sounded like she was at her wit's end. "Oh, I went too far," she murmured, flipping through the pages. "No! Too far back! Um— 'The easiest way to determine if you were successful in creating a minion is to strongly wish for them to spin around three times and tell an especially hilarious joke. Saying the request aloud will be more effective, as it will clarify your consciousness. Of course, it is ideal if the subject can hear your voice. In most cases, after spinning around three times, the subject will experience discomfort because they are unable to come up with a joke. If they do this, then that is proof you have found yourself a suitable minion. Should your subject come up with a hilariously funny joke, then it is recommended you give them a career in comedy. If they do not even spin around, then they have not been made your minion.' There you have it… Spin around three times."

"You spin around. Three thousand times."

"Um— 'In instances where the subject has not become your minion after biting into them for three minutes, then please consider the following causes: One, your spit still lacks the substance to create minions. This is because you are too young. Please wait until you turn fifteen. Two, are you really of Sacred Blood? Are you sure you're not a Japanese person who thinks they're Sacred Blood? Please see a medical professional for delusions of grandeur. Three, some other exceptional case.' This can't be. I am a wonderful high school student who just turned seventeen last month…"

"Are you sure you're not a wonderful middle school student who just turned thirteen the other day? You are way shorter than the average high school girl."

She punched him straight in the stomach.

"Guh… You can't just punch people without warning…"

"It's fine. Your face is in perfect condition."

"That's not the problem!"

"Ahhhh! He's so quick to retort… This can't… N-no, wait…"

The girl named Shiren Fuyukura crouched to the floor, cradling her head.

Ryouta wasn't quite sure what was going on, but she seemed to be shocked to find he wasn't her minion. He wondered if he should sympathize with her, but she had already bit and punched him, so he decided to stay neutral. "I dunno what's going on here, but I need to get going home. I'll walk to Akinomiya Station. I honestly should probably take you to court for this, but it looks like you have enough problems as it is, so I'll let you go."

He was tired of dealing with her. They could barely communicate.

"Huh? The JR lines aren't in operation," Shiren Fuyukura said with a blank look.

"Ugh. Was there a cave-in along one of the tunnels, then? Well, there are buses from the station that go to Oshiro anyway."

"The public bus to Oshiro is out of service, too. The only ones running are domestic Imperial lines."

"No way… Well, I guess I could walk for four hours, and I'd reach Oshiro by then…"

"No, you have no way to leave the Empire. All the roads are closed."

And that was when Ryouta finally realized something was amiss.

"Wait, where are we?"

"5-25 4-chome, Midori-dai, Sacred Blood Empire, postcode 4-238561."

"What was that after Midori-dai?"

"Sacred Blood Empire."

Ryouta decided to get a grasp on the situation first; going home would come later.

He sat opposite Shiren Fuyukura at the table. She had cushions laid out for them to sit on, and there was also a cup of tomato juice on the table.

"First, Fuyukura, why did you bite my neck?"

"Don't call me Fuyukura. You are my minion, so—"

"**Half-pint. Middle schooler. Brat. Midpubescent.** I'll call you whatever I want."

"F-Fuyukura's fine… I bit your neck to gain a minion for myself. It's said that those of Sacred Blood are considered of age when they have their own minion. If you still don't have your own minion when you reach high school, people start mocking you—*Ba-ha-ha-ha, grooooss! Only middle schoolers don't have their own minions!* And I guess there really aren't very many high schoolers without a minion."

"Wait. Stop using words I don't know in your answers. Sacred Blood? Is that some new band or something? I don't really know anything about current events; I don't watch the news."

"Wait, really? Are you serious? You're Japanese, and you don't know about the Sacred Blooded?" Shiren looked at him as if she'd just seen an alien.

He felt a twinge of regret, wondering if he'd just made a fool of himself with that question.

"Question: What's the name of the current prime minister of Japan?"

"Koichiro Hirokawa."

"He resigned four whole months ago."

"Are you serious…? My info only ever updates once every six months…"

The girl looked at Ryouta with pity. "I'm sorry; it's not like you can enforce common knowledge. Everyone's unique, but it doesn't mean everyone has to be the best. Yes, you're just as fine as you are."

"O-okay, your reaction is more than insulting; you're acting sorry for me… Am I really that out of the loop?"

"Listen…I didn't expect there to be any Japanese people who were really this clueless, so I'm not sure if you'll believe me, but let me start from the beginning. Five months ago in April, the Sacred Blooded brought the Japanese city of Akinomiya under its control and turned it into Empire territory."

"You're kidding!"

"I'm serious," she replied immediately.

"Um, so basically, Akinomiya became a sovereign nation about half a year ago... Is that what you mean?"

"Right. But of course, Japan still won't recognize this country's independence, so I'm apparently considered a Japanese citizen under Japanese law. We're being forced under a 'one country, two systems' policy. That's why the Self-Defense Force isn't able to enter, and we can keep our peace."

It sounded like these Sacred Blood people had taken over the town, and Ryouta had wandered in by chance. To think his ignorance of current events would result in such tragedy...

"Hmm, you appear to be in pain. Don't you like tomato juice? Would you prefer blood?"

"No, I'm *definitely* okay with tomato juice— Wait, what? Your people have *Blood* in the name, and you suddenly came and bit me, which means— No way... But wait, isn't it weird that you can substitute tomato juice for blood...? But..."

This was something he definitely did not want to think about...

"You Japanese call us vampires. I think it's much too rude to liken us to silly fairy-tale creatures. Our emperor is currently filing a complaint with the UN that it's a terribly discriminatory word. We have a proud history and tradition over two thousand years old! It was all torn to pieces after years of terrible suppression, but we still lived on in secret, and we have been waiting for our rallying moment since. And then finally this year, we rose under the Emperor's command and took Akinomiya! There are currently forty thousand Sacred Blooded and ten thousand minions living in the Empire."

Ryouta had been completely oblivious to Japan's tumultuous situation.

"Okay... Then can you tell me more about these minions you keep mentioning?"

"It's essentially what you think of when you hear the word: When a Sacred Blooded bites a human, that human can be put to work. Apparently, this happens because of something in our saliva that enters the bloodstream when we bite them, but I don't know the details."

"You get bit by a vampire and then turned into their underling..."

Ryouta mentally compared this with the stories of vampires he'd often heard before.

As a test, he straightened both of his index fingers, held one vertically and one horizontally across it, and shoved them at Shiren.

"How's this, Fuyukura? Anything?"

"You have horizontal line AB with vertical line CD across the midpoint, creating ninety-degree angles."

"Wait, you're not scared of the cross…?"

"That's an old wives' tale. We historically never got along with Christians, so we just get irritated when we see the cross. But I suppose they would hide such a black mark on their own history."

So they did have a violent history.

"Huh. Okay, then how about garlic?"

"Personal fave. Gets my blood going."

"There really isn't much unique about you guys… Isn't there anything that makes you special?"

"We get hardier and stronger for a little while after drinking blood."

Shiren held out her arms and posed, flexing her biceps. There wasn't much muscle there to flex, though.

"I'm not very good at physical activity, if I do say so myself…"

"Yeah, you really didn't need to say it yourself. But forget about that— Do the Sacred Blooded have any particular weaknesses?"

"We hate slimy things…"

"Slimy things?"

"Yams, natto, *nameko* mushrooms, okra—we get hives just looking at the stuff… We hate liquid soap, too, so we buy the kind that comes out in foam… And a while ago on TV, there was some sort of series on cooking with slugs, and yeah, no. No thank you. If someone told me to eat one of those, I'd probably just bite off my tongue and die."

"I think that's just a personal preference of yours."

"Okay then, would *you* eat a slug if someone told you to?!"

"No, definitely not! Wait, we're off topic here! I don't care about what you have to say about slimy stuff!"

They'd gotten off track, so it was time to regroup. In short:

"…Are you really a vampire, Fuyukura?"

When he called her a vampire again, Shiren's eyebrows twitched upward.

"Don't use that word! It's rude! Those spooky creatures in stories are just based off a real people who drink blood! We're the original! You've got it backward!"

Well, what he got from that was that these Sacred Blooded people were an actual thing.

But hold on.

"Then why don't I have to obey you, even after you bit me?"

He could read the panic in her face: *Oh no, why'd he have to ask that?*

At least she was aware of it.

"You see, when the humidity rises over a certain percent, the compounds that control humans sometimes don't work effectively. The reason this happens is because bacteria proliferates in high humidity and blocks the crucial compounds. So then you might think dry winter days are better, but if it gets too cold, then that can hinder the activation of the enzymes, so that's not great, either. Also, they say that for ages, it's always been hardest to create minions on days of omen, *butsumetsu*, but easiest on days of auspice, *taian*. I think that's rather unscientific, but I suspect there's some surprising facet of truth to this old tale. I think it's shortsighted to sneer at your own past."

Wondering if today was an auspicious day, Ryouta reached out to the book next to Shiren.

The *My First Minion* book.

His eyes settled on what he was looking for.

In instances where the subject has not become your minion after biting into them for three minutes, then please consider the following causes:

1. Your spit still lacks the substance to create minions. This is because you are too young. Please wait until you turn fifteen.

"This basically says you're still too much of a kid to make any minions, Fuyukura."

"You don't have to say it out loud… This is embarrassing…" Shiren leaned over and planted her face onto the table. Her pigtails sprawled across it like worms.

Ryouta felt a little bad for her; he was slightly more sympathetic this time. Still, he was glad he hadn't been made into a minion. He found himself placing his hand on his chest in relief.

At least the girl in front of him wasn't harmful. He had nothing to be afraid of. She was just a girl.

Wait…just a *girl*?

"Hey, can I check something with you, Fuyukura? What do you think of when you see me?"

"Upset that I couldn't turn you into a minion, obviously. Shameful is the Sacred Blooded who does not make a minion of the human before them…"

"No, not like that. Like, your heart clenching, or you can't stop thinking about me—what I mean is a crush or something."

"Okay, you can only be so self-conscious. I suppose if I had to say, you have a nice face, maybe even a feminine face… But your personality is hideous." Shiren glared at Ryouta with a *This guy's the worst* kind of look.

"No way!" Ryouta placed his hands on the girl's shoulders and yanked her into a hug.

"Gah! Wh-wh-what are you doing?! I'm the only one in the house here! You're the worst! Japanese people are all dogs! I hate you!"

Having suddenly been pulled into a hug, Shiren's face instantly turned bright red. But Ryouta paid that no mind and held her tighter.

"S… Stop… I know I'm the one who took you in here, but I had no intentions of this… At least give me a moment to prepare…" Tears were welling in Shiren's eyes.

"Fuyukura, what do you think of me? Be honest."

"I… I hate you, obviously! Why would you think I'd be happy you're forcing me to do this?! You're the worst! I hate you!"

"You hate me? You mean you don't see me as a love interest? And if you're thinking *I-it's not like I* LIKE *you or anything!* it still counts as romance, by the way."

"Don't make me laugh! What makes you think I'd have feelings for a creep who says gross stuff like that?!"

"YESSSSSSSSSSSSSSSS!!!!!"

Overjoyed, Ryouta couldn't stop himself from springing into the air.

If this were an apartment, the downstairs neighbors would have complained about the noise.

"Wait... You're happy that a girl tells you she hates you? Are you some kind of masochist? But you have such a nice face... I guess the heavens don't give with both hands."

"No! It's all because of my gramps's spell! He made me irresistibly attractive to girls, but it doesn't seem like there's any effect on the Sacred Blooded!"

"I've never heard of any such perverse spell..." Shiren gave Ryouta an exasperated look.

"All right, I'm gonna live here in the Sacred Blood Empire! We're cut off from Japan, and there's no way to go back anyway, right? So I'll live here as a human in this new world! I'll live a good and honest life!"

"Calm down! You can't just start living here that easily!"

"I don't care how hard it gets; it'll be way better than Japan! My sister attacks me at home, my classmates attack me at school, college girls drag me into their cars if I ever walk down an empty street—do you understand my pain? Japan is a real-life dystopia to me, a world of crumbling moral values!"

As long as there were women in the world, Ryouta could never live in peace. He had honestly and seriously been contemplating living out his future on a deserted island.

But the majority of the population of this country were of Sacred Blood, and they weren't affected by the spell.

"I can finally have the right to life prescribed in the Japanese constitution!"

He had to strike while the iron was hot. Ryouta was already gearing up to leave the girl's house.

"I'll find an apartment somewhere. There's probably a real estate agent in front of the station, right? I'd have to get a job to pay rent, but I think it's better that way. Thanks for everything!"

But suddenly, his legs grew heavy, and the bell around his neck chimed. Shiren was clinging to his legs.

"Sorry, but you'll have to do the cooking and cleaning and weeding all on your own."

"Stop! Don't be so hasty!"

"Well, I'll do it if you pay me over nine hundred yen an hour. I do think my cooking is pretty good."

"Calm down and listen to me! You'll be bitten immediately if you go outside!"

"Bitten?"

"The Sacred Blooded's sense of smell can distinguish their compatriots and human minions from other types of humans. Basically, the second you step outside, you'll look like the perfect candidate to become a minion! Don't blame me if you end up the minion of some brawny, serious, stern bloodsucker!"

At Shiren's description, a horrible image appeared in his head.

"Right, you came up to me because you found me, didn't you?"

"Yeah. It smelled like human, so I took out *My First Minion* because I bring it with me everywhere, and then I approached you. I also questioned you to make sure you were the right type of human to make a minion, remember?"

"You're strangely conscientious for someone who subjugates humans..."

Ryouta finally understood why she had been asking such shady questions. She was trying to make sure he was okay with leaving Japan to be a minion.

But in this situation, that still didn't change the fact that going outside would be essentially advertising himself as a potential victim.

"Are you telling me that the second I leave this house, the locals will start coming after me like I'm a million yen just walking around?"

"The Sacred Blooded aren't barbarians, nor are we hyenas that flock to dead carcasses. But I think you are more or less correct."

"This is the worst..."

Feeling his energy draining away, Ryouta crumpled to the floor on the spot.

He hated that for a fraction of a second, he believed he'd found paradise. He wouldn't even be able to leave the house at this rate.

"So…what would happen to my consciousness if someone did turn me into a minion?"

If he ended up like a robot with no free will, he'd be in serious trouble.

"You think we're pure evil, don't you? You won't lose your own consciousness. The most your master could force you to do is to come to her vicinity, and no more."

It wasn't as severe as he thought.

"Some people refuse to do any cooking, cleaning, laundry, or anything else and do nothing but eat," Ryouta mused. "According to them, they are excellent servants who guard their master's house. Actually, that's not unlike a butler living in a mansion."

"Then I guess you can pretty much do what you want, as long as you don't want to go anywhere. But if you were the minion of some nutjob, you couldn't ever run away, because they'd just call you back…"

Ryouta suddenly found himself at a loss, thinking of his whole life ahead of him.

………

He was in such despair that his mind went blank.

He'd thought he'd had it rough when just women came after him, but now he found himself in a world where he would be attacked by both men and women.

If this was the alternative, Japan would be much better.

"What am I supposed to do?" Ryouta asked Shiren, lowering his head. There was no one else he could rely on here.

"Clean this room and make me some omelet rice."

"I was an idiot for asking you."

"Um, well, I have Internet here in my house, so you could stay here and play MMOs until they consume your mind?"

"You mean I've really gotten myself stuck… But I guess…this is all my fault, since I never look at the news. You have to pay close attention to what's going on in the world around you… If you don't, you're always open to exploitation…"

If he were anywhere within walking distance of the Sea of Trees on Mount Fuji, he would've been compelled to go straight there. But he couldn't even leave.

On the other hand, Shiren's expression suddenly lit up. "Oh, that's right—I know what we can do! This would be a win-win situation. Just wait here!"

It looked as if she'd gotten a spark of inspiration, and she left the room. He could hear her mumbling to herself in the other room: "This isn't it; that's not it… Here it is!"

She came right back, hiding something behind her back.

"There is one way you can walk freely within the Empire and live as a normal human."

"Huh, okay…" Ryouta's gaze snapped upward to his ray of light…! But when his eyes reached Shiren's expression, he saw a crafty grin on her face—and a metal chain in her hands. "W-w-wait, seriously?!"

"Just place this on your collar."

That reminded him he was still wearing it.

"You will spend each day with the collar on, and when you go outside, I'll attach this chain and walk around with you. Everyone will then recognize you as my minion."

"What kind of kinky crap is this?!"

"But you *can* go outside like this; I guarantee it. The Sacred Blood Empire Civil Code Article Sixty-Seven states: 'If one has yet to carry out the minion contract, they must clearly demonstrate by any means their intention to make the subject their minion in the future.' So it might be a little sketchy with just a collar, but as long as the candidate for the master is at the other end of the chain, then no one can touch you."

That sounded reasonable. This way, she could take him to a safe place. If he could get to the base of the mountain, the game was his.

"Thank you! Now I can go home! I was thinking about how terrible it would be if I'd been taken in by some weirdo, but I take it back! You're practically a saint!"

Ryouta got on his knees and prostrated himself to her. He needed Shiren's help to go home.

"Excuse me? Did I ever say I'd let you go home?" she asked coolly from above.

When he looked up, he saw a wicked smile on Shiren's face. A villainous smile.

"What? ...Aren't you pretending to be my future master with the chain so you can take me somewhere I won't be attacked? You're not helping me get back to Japan?"

"No," she responded instantly. "Erm, your name's Ryouta Asagiri, right? Ryouta, my gift to you is the life of a human in Empire lands. As the minion (candidate) of Shiren Fuyukura, that is."

"You're saying...I should promise to be your minion...?"

"Exactly. If you do, then I can guarantee your safety. It goes without saying that you will serve me both in and out of the house, though."

"Urgh... She's taking advantage of me."

"I'm not saying it's impossible to pull off. You can leave this house and run if you want. There aren't many people in the residential area in the mountain, and you might be able to escape without being found. And then you might be able to return to Japan. But if you leave, I'll report you."

Man, this girl doesn't have the word mercy *in her vocabulary...*

"But I suppose even if you ended up caught by another Sacred Blooded, one of those big-breasted women you love so much might make you her minion instead, so you might think it's not so bad after all."

"I never said I was into that; don't put words in my mouth."

"Oh, and there's this seriously buff older man living nearby, and he's apparently looking for a minion. His motto, by the way, is *Gays of a feather*."

Ryouta could physically feel his blood draining, to the point that he finally understood where the expression came from.

"Please let me live here for just a little while longer..." Ryouta bowed his head.

He felt humiliated, but it was the only way for him to survive.

But wait, it wasn't like he was going to turn into her minion straightaway. He could just slip out and escape when he had a chance.

"You weren't just thinking about slipping away when you had a chance and stealing my money on your way out, were you?"

She was mostly right, but she was adding to his crimes.

"That's not enough. Get on your knees and say, *Please allow me to live in your grand abode and serve you as your humble minion, Lady Shiren Fuyukura.*"

"I'm gonna make you cry one of these days, I swear it. I'll make you grovel and say, *I'm so sorry, Ryouta Asagiri, sir.*"

Please allow me to live in your grand abode and serve you as your humble minion, Lady Shiren Fuyukura.

"I think you may have switched your thoughts and your show of obedience…"

"Crap! I was so mad I forgot!"

"…Very well. You will soon realize how magnificent I am as a master, and you will worship me. Now stand."

When he lifted his gaze, Shiren took Ryouta's hand and pulled him to his feet.

"Ryouta, starting today, you will faithfully serve me as my minion."

"She's calling me by my first name as if she's earned the right…" It was inevitable, but it still irritated him. "I will serve you well, Lady Fuyukura."

"Just Shiren is fine."

He was surprised to hear she was okay with that.

"Then…Shiren."

"Oh, I wanted you to call me Lady Shiren, but…I suppose I'll let it slide. Shiren is fine."

"Shiren, hmm. You know, that's kind of a cute name."

"You know, the official way to write my name originally came from a shortened version of *leonine purgatory.*"

"What are you, a creature in an action comic?!"

"Anyway. It's a pleasure, Ryouta." Shiren held out her hand.

Guess I'll be deferential this time. "No, the pleasure is mine, Shiren."

When he shook her hand, he found that it was smaller than he thought.

He finally realized that this was his first time shaking hands with a woman who had no ulterior motives.

He didn't mind handshakes like this.

There was a clear master-servant relationship between them, though.

"Yay! Now I have my own minion!" Shiren's excitement was clear in her voice, and the unbridled joy in her eyes matched her innocent smile. "You are mine starting today, Ryouta. Forever and ever!"

I never agreed to forever.

Well, if she's gonna be this happy about it, then maybe it'll be worth serving her for a bit.

While he was talking to her, another forty-three new texts had come from Kiyomizu.

He deleted them all.

©Hiroki Ozaki

Shiren Fuyukura

I am Ryouta's master—tidy, sweet, and the most beautiful girl in the Empire.

That's a bit much!

EPISODE 2
**LET'S LEARN ABOUT SACRED BLOODED LIFE
AND CULTURE!**

"Oh, long time no see, Ryouta. Although I suppose this is a dream."

Ouka was smiling at Ryouta. If Ouka said he was dreaming, he was.

She stood before him, and she looked old enough to be a high school student now. Ryouta had known her only up to fourth grade.

"Why are you coming into my dreams, Ouka? What do you want?" Ryouta responded, his gaze trained on his feet. He was still shy around his first crush, even when he was asleep.

"W-well, this is your dream, after all, and it's not going to have any effect on my reality, and it's not like I know the truth of this dream, so that's why it's a very low risk on my part to show you mercy."

That was really roundabout.

She then averted her gaze. "What I am trying to say is, you can kiss me if you want."

"Wuh… Wh-wuuuuh?"

"Ugh, your flustered reaction isn't exactly attractive. This is an exception, okay? An exception. This is a dream anyway, and it seems like you're in serious trouble out in the real world… Come on, do it quickly, or you'll wake up!"

So it was a dream after all. The kanji characters that made up Ouka's name really did fit her perfectly: a regal flower. She never acted shy like this. But if he could kiss her…

"Are you sure it's okay?" Ryouta slowly approached her.

"Don't make me repeat myself. It might be a dream, but I'm still embarrassed about this!"

Ryouta placed both hands on her shoulders. He then gradually leaned forward to press his lips to hers—aaand right when he thought he was in the clear, Ouka bit him. *On the neck.*

"GYAAAAAAAAAAAAAAAAAAAAAAAA!!"

When he woke up, he found teeth deep in his neck.

But of course, they belonged to Shiren.

"What are you doing...? Can you stop biting me for a hot second?"

"You're up. Well, I thought I could make you my minion today..."

Now that she mentioned it, he'd fallen unconscious after she bit him yesterday, but nothing particular happened today. He must be building some immunity to it.

"You're the reason I dreamed about—! ...*Sigh*, no, never mind."

He was embarrassed to say he had dreamed about his first crush, so he didn't. Man, what a waste of a dream that turned out to be...

"Hmm? What's the matter, Ryouta? You look like a high school baseball player who's had his dreams dashed."

"No, it's nothing, really..."

"Either way, a minion must offer a comfortable wake-up for his master. To have to be woken up is an enormous dereliction of duty. Be ready—for all the days I wake up first, I will take a bite out of you."

"Easy for you to say, but that means you're threatening my life first thing in the morning!"

"It is now time for breakfast, then. Get ready, quickly. Oh yes, you need this, and this."

She clipped on the chain to his collar.

"All right then, let's go to the dining room!"

Shiren gripped the chain as she went down the stairs.

"This is just plain slavery... I should get out of here soon... Gah! Slow down on the stairs! I'm gonna fall!"

The day had only just begun, and Ryouta already found himself sighing.

* * *

They had last night's leftovers for breakfast—miso soup and some side dishes.

"Yum! You have a talent for cooking, Ryouta. Allow me to praise you!"

"More that you're just really bad at it. I can't believe you almost put ketchup in the soup."

Ryouta had made most of last night's dinner. He'd always had a knack for cooking. He was basically freeloading off her, so he had planned to at least do the housework.

"Yes, this is delicious! The salt on this fried mackerel is absolutely divine! More rice!"

He scooped her some seconds from the rice cooker beside him. As the one who did all the cooking, he found it worth it in the end to have someone genuinely tell him she enjoyed it.

"You sure eat a lot, Shiren."

"Only because it's so good!"

"Seriously, aren't you going to put on some weight if you wolf it down like that?"

Shiren's chopsticks froze in midair, and it became so quiet that Ryouta wondered if he'd suddenly gained the power to stop time.

"Ha...ha-ha-ha..."

A dry laugh slipped from Shiren's lips. Her face was smiling, but her eyes were dead cold.

Whoops, he'd crossed a line he shouldn't have.

"Oh dear, this will not do, Ryouta. It is the most taboo of taboos to speak of weight gain in front of women. If you said this in front of the Emperor, she would have to resort to violence and punch you in the face. Well, I won't act so aggressively. I'll just poke at you in warning."

"Ha-ha... I'm sorry. I won't talk about getting fat in front of you anymore."

"Then allow me to caution you."

Shiren dug her pointer finger into Ryouta...

...'s right eye.

"Graaaaaaaaaaagh! That's my eye, my eye!!"

Ryouta writhed, pressing a hand to his face. It was such a strange sight, someone might be inspired to upload a video of it and call it "The True Meaning of Agony."

"*Gasp...gasp...* What the heck are you doing?! That defies all the laws of common sense!"

"As I promised, I simply poked you in warning. I'll go for both of your eyes next time. If you don't like the idea of that, then slap some glasses on and become a glasses character! Do you understand me now? This is why you don't talk about getting fat in front of girls. That would be like telling a boy that...uh..."

From the way the conversation was going, it sounded as if she was going to give an example here, but she faltered. Her face was red for some reason.

"Don't tell me you got so embarrassed at your own example you can't even say it?"

"Shut up! Th-th-th-th-that's not it at all!"

She dug her finger into his eye again. (Don't try this at home, kids.)

"Aaaaaaaaaaaaaaaaaaaaaaaaaaaaaaaaaaagh! I can see my ancestors...!!"

Afterward, Ryouta profoundly reflected on all the types of violence in the world.

He turned on the TV to the news, also to change the mood.

It looked as if they were just in time for the typical horoscope hour that came with the morning news.

"And now for the Sacred Blood News satellite, our segment on today's blood-type horoscope. The luckiest people today will be those with blood type B! Drinking will give you energy, and you may receive special praise from your boss. Next luckiest will be those of blood type O! You might find a trinket you've lost if you drink! Next on the list is—"

"Hold it! Change the channel!"

Other channels featured shows such as *Morning Bloodpool*, *Good Bloody Morning*, and other news broadcasts with names that did nothing to reassure him. Of course, Ryouta had never seen these before.

"Why are you being so loud first thing in the morning?! Where are your table manners? I'll poke you again."

"All these bloody news channels— *Blech!*"

There was a tug on the chain attached to his collar, and Ryouta retched. This was difficult during mealtime.

"Be quiet, servant. This is the land of the Sacred Blooded, so of course the programs on TV will be for the Sacred Blooded. But never fear—we have the broadcast rights to popular shows from Japan, so they air episodes of *Precure* and *S——e-san* and special Friday night showings of Miyazaki films."

"Why are they all anime?"

"There are no companies within Empire territory that create animations yet. You could also say our population isn't large enough to support the industry, so we have no choice but to buy the rights. Mm, yes, the food is delicious. This just confirms my feelings that a traditional Sacred Blood breakfast is much better than just plain bread!"

"I don't know if I would call this traditional Sacred Blood food…"

"This food isn't exclusive to Japan, you know. It's our time-honored cuisine as well, and for a reason. It would take a good three hours to explain about the creation of traditional dishes and Sacred Blooded involvement, so we'll leave that for another time."

Everything about these people was setting off his bullshit detector.

"Huh. I was just wondering, by the way, but is that your uniform?" he asked.

Shiren was wearing a blazer, which was clearly a part of a school uniform. "Yes. I am a high schooler, after all. Year Two, Class Three of the Sacred Blood First High School. Hmph!"

She suddenly pulled on his chain, and Ryouta's face slammed into the table.

"You were just thinking, *You don't look like a second-year student at all. You look like a sixth grader*, weren't you?"

"I never said anything like that! Stop using your master privileges so sudden— Guh!"

She pulled on his chain again. "Stop talking back to me like that. You will be my minion one day, Ryouta. You're infinitely close to becoming my minion for real. I'm not asking you to call me *Lady* Shiren, but at least be polite. If you need ideas for softening your language, I can suggest some stock phrases such as 'the great' or 'even greater than Venus, the goddess of beauty.'"

"You are way too full of yourself, Lady Shiren. You need to adopt a more reserved attitude, Lady Shiren. You're very short—are you sure you don't have a condition, Lady Shiren?"

"I'm going to poke both of your eyes in five hours."

"Please don't; you're freaking me out! If you're going to, then just do it now! I always eat my least favorite foods first!"

"It's almost time. Get changed, Ryouta. I will take the chain off you only for now."

"Wait, I'm going to school, too?"

That was unexpected. He was under the impression he'd be forced to stay home and do all the cleaning.

"The Sacred Blooded have an obligation to give their minions the education they want, and minions have the right to the education they want within reason. A minion without intelligence is an embarrassment to his master. That's why you will graduate from high school and get into a good university. You will get into Tokyo University, even if it kills you. And no dinner for you if you are not in the top ten of your graduating class."

"My 'rights' started to sound a little compulsory there…"

Well, beats staying home all day and doing chores, Ryouta thought. He'd have to do them when he got home anyway, though.

"Indeed, you should thank me. And I want to parade my potential minion around at school."

"I think I just heard you muttering something under your breath there."

"Just your imagination. Now go, quickly! Your change of clothes is already waiting for you in your room!"

Public High School No. 1, Established to Nurture the Talent That Will Create Our Noble Future

The school's full name was long.

"This is my school: Public High School No. 1, Probably Established to Just Inflict Pain on Us and I Wish They Loved Us More."

"You only got the very first part of that right."

"Oh no! I thought I memorized that for my quiz!"

"They quiz you on your school name? What kind of school is this…?"

The walk was about fifteen minutes from the house to the school gates.

It was just an ordinary public high school; only the name had been changed. As the two stood before the gates, the flow of students into the school passed by them and into the school grounds. To be honest, their school uniforms looked just like Japanese uniforms at first glance.

Every time a student passed the duo, they stared and whispered "What is that?" and "Ewww!"

Ryouta heard all of it. He felt like he'd become some kind of pervert.

He always attracted the attention of girls in Japan, but this kind of attention was a first.

"Heh-heh. It seems my minion (candidate) has caught everyone's attention! My minion (candidate) will rule the world in the next five years as its supreme overlord!"

"Stop! Don't pick out my path in life without telling me! And they're not looking at me because I'm your minion! Let's just get to class, okay?"

"Is it my beauty, then?"

"Don't interpret it so optimistically. First, this collar!"

Ryouta poked at the collar on his neck. The chain rattled.

He'd walked through town to school, being led on a collar by a girl. This was totally perverted. Plus, to make matters worse, the collar was only one of the things she'd made him wear.

"And what are these clothes?! These aren't normal!"

Ryouta swished the skirt he was wearing.

He had on the same girls' uniform that Shiren wore. Of course, that included the skirt on the bottom.

"What else am I supposed to do? I don't have a male uniform in my house. I would never make you wear my clothes; I'm not a deviant. And the only ally I could borrow a uniform from was Tamaki."

Sure, without any close male friends, she probably wouldn't have been able to borrow any.

"Then at least let me come to school in the regular clothes I was wearing yesterday…"

"They were rather sweaty since you had been hiking in the mountains for hours. If you wore them, then everyone would remember you as the sweaty boy."

That wouldn't have been good, either, but it would've been better than coming to school in the girls' uniform. But it was too late.

"Still, it looks better on you than I thought. You have a feminine face, so you sort of look like a girl if you squint."

"Oh yes, that's exactly how it looks, heh-heh."

Ryouta heard an unfamiliar voice, and a moment later, the unfamiliar girl who belonged to it appeared.

She had long, glossy black hair. The first impression he got was that she was a traditionally beautiful girl, trim and tidy. She was so beautiful that a foreigner would've praised her as the epitome of Japanese charm.

"You look like a girl from behind, but your strides are a little too wide when you walk," she remarked.

"Right. And you should keep your arms closer to your center," Shiren added. "If they go too far forward, you look fatter."

"Okay, I don't need your advice, and I'm not really interested in learning how to cross-dress. And who is this?"

There was too much for him to comment on, so he went in order.

"Oh, this is my classmate and only comrade, Tamaki Shijou."

"'Only'? How lonely are you? Wait, so this uniform belongs to you!"

"Hello, I'm Tamaki Shijou. Yes, that uniform is mine. Oh, a boy is wearing it… This is too much; I didn't know it'd be used for such a fetishistic activity…"

When she realized what was happening, tears began welling in Tamaki Shijou's eyes.

"No! You're completely misreading this! I swear!"

"Don't tell me you did a-a-all sorts of unmentionable things wearing the uniform? I'm so scared; what if I can't wear it anymore?! And it's brand-new, too! My third mother bought that for me before she died!"

"I haven't done anything weird, okay?! I just put it on before leaving for school! And why did you have to bring up something so serious?!"

Shiren tapped Ryouta on the back and leaned over to whisper, "Tell her you like the library committee armband she's wearing."

Now that she mentioned it, he noticed the red armband around her right arm. The character for *book* was written large on it.

"Nice arm band there, Shijou."

"Oh, I'm so sorry for doubting you. Anyone who compliments me for the armband is never a bad person, eh-heh-heh." Tamaki immediately stopped crying and smiled.

"Tamaki will forgive anyone for anything if you compliment her armband. She has a strong persecution complex, but she's reliable."

"Okay. She seems kind of weird, but she's a good person. Oh, my name's Ryouta."

"I am a worthless being with a life like old dirt, but it is nice to meet you, Ryouta." Tamaki smiled kindly and gently.

"I think calling yourself dirt might be too much, but... Nice to meet you, too."

Tamaki's smile was mature and calm, as you might expect from an upperclassman. There was a magnanimity about her that suggested she'd listen to any of your worries.

After all's said and done, Shiren still is pretty cute, so I guess Sacred Blooded girls are generally high quality, Ryouta thought silently.

"Tamaki is really important. She's like the mediator in the class, and she's on the library committee. Since we just established ourselves as a country, the collection of books hasn't been organized yet, so she works on the weekends, too."

"Whoa, that's really important work!"

Since she was coming to school flaunting her armband, she must really love books.

"It's not much. It's best for utter trash such as myself to do the jobs no one else wants to do," Tamaki said, her expression warm.

"You're a good person, Shijou, but I think you're being a little *too* modest..." People didn't usually call themselves lowly dirt and utter trash. "But you do love books, don't you?"

"Books are heavy and cumbersome and a waste of paper resources, but such nonsense is perfect for me. And heavier, thicker books can become weapons in times of need."

"I can't interpret anything you've said as a love for books. Is it okay for you to be on the library committee?!"

"Tamaki's just a little negative. Don't worry about it. Oh, and the official meaning of her name is 'mourning of the serpent demon.'"

"Oh, stop, don't say that; that's embarrassing!" Tamaki hid her face with her bag.

"Your official meaning was 'something something purgatory,' wasn't it, Shiren? Do all the Sacred Blooded have to have these RPG-sounding names…?"

"Well, I have some committee work I must get to. I'll see you around." Like a nobleman's daughter, Tamaki gracefully made off for the school building.

"I guess we should get going, too." Shiren tugged at the chain attached to the collar.

"You don't have to pull. I'm getting kind of nervous."

To Ryouta, this was like transferring to a new school. In short, his high school debut.

"But I didn't think I'd be debuting in the girl's uniform and a collar…"

He vowed to make Shiren buy a male uniform for him.

"This is my minion (candidate)!"

The second they entered the classroom, Shiren was yelling, and his debut was an instant failure.

"Well? I know most of you still don't have minions. I knew I would never be able to hide my noble blood. Aren't I magnificent? Aren't I amazing? You may applaud me as much as you want."

"I knew Shiren was cringy, but now she's being cringy even in class…"

The students in the classroom started loudly discussing Shiren and Ryouta.

"Wow, she found a minion already. Sounds like he's still only a candidate, though."

"That was fast. People like that sure grow up quick, don't they?"

Also—

"Wait, Fuyukura lives alone, right? That means…"

"Stop, don't go there. I think there's only about a two percent chance that they have an innocent relationship."

And—

"Why is he dressed in the girls' uniform?"

"I mean, people are into all sorts of stuff, right? Bet he's a drag queen."

"But he's not wearing makeup."

"Yeah, if he's gonna go for it, he should go for it."

Uniform talk aside, they were talking about him in a way that honestly creeped him out. It looked as if high school here had something else in common with Japan—putting teenaged boys and girls under the same roof was a recipe for conflict.

The silver lining to this whole tragedy was that none of them came to talk to Shiren directly.

But Ryouta wasn't just an object of observation—he was scoping out the class himself.

"The Sacred Blooded aren't really that much different from regular humans," he murmured softly. The students in the class just looked like typical high school kids.

Since Shiren had Internet, he'd looked up the Sacred Blooded online the night before and found real articles on the whole uproar about their independence back in April.

Man, this was big. It was really bad that I didn't know anything about it...

Those articles mentioned all kinds of information, such as how the Empire and Japan were holding negotiations in secret and how they were still uncertain about border lines and all that. Not even Japan could stay quiet if an independent country was established within its borders.

"Okay, everyone, take your seats."

A balding middle-aged teacher entered the room.

"Fuyukura's minion, why don't you introduce yourself now? And go buy yourself a boys' uniform at the school store during the break. You can pay for it tomorrow."

"Oh good, I'm glad the teacher's understanding..."

He went up to the front, accompanied by Shiren as she was still holding the chain. She probably wanted to show him off.

"Hello, I'm Ryouta Asagiri, I'm sevente— Guh! Bluh!"

The chain suddenly pulled him downward.

"If you make the same mistake again, I'm pulling you another six inches!"

"Did I say something bad?!"

"You are still unaware of your position as a minion, so I'll introduce you for you. This is my minion, Ryouta Fuyukura. He's in the same year of school as us, so he's transferred here. He's happy to meet you all."

"Huh? We have the same last name, which makes us sound like we're marrie— Gruuuugh! Buh!"

She pulled on the chain three times harder than she did before.

"Don't be such an embarrassment! Minions take the same last name as their master!"

"I never heard about that, so I didn't know… You coulda killed me there…"

And so, class started.

First period, math.

The material was practically the same as what was being taught at Ryouta's school, and the textbook was nearly identical to a Japanese one. And Shiren, by the way, was asleep.

Second period, English.

The material in this class was almost the same as well, but the example sentences were a little odd.

"Now, why don't we have Ryouta Fuyukura, our transfer student, read this one?"

The female teacher (probably in her early- to midthirties) nominated Ryouta, so he read the passage. Except his pronunciation made it sound as if he was just speaking Japanese—it was terrible.

"*Hiroshi: Hello. Jim: Hello. I am from America. Hiroshi: I am from Sacred Blood. Jim (groveling for some reason): Oh, you are great. You are the champion. You are the creative master of space—* Hey, what is he talking about?! This is ridiculous? 'The creative master of space'?!"

"Be quiet and continue reading, Fuyukura."

"*Your country's emperor is a very, very cute girl. She is more beautiful than Cleopatra, Yang Yuhuan, Ono no Komachi…* Hey, the Emperor sounds pretty full of herself."

"Speaking ill of the Emperor is a jailable offense!"

Since this was an empire, their emperor would be a real head of state, but she sounded awfully strange.

Besides the issues with the English passages, it was an unexpectedly normal class. Despite being vampires, they didn't drink one another's blood at all. In fact, that would only subjugate them to one another, so drinking the blood of other Sacred Blooded was prohibited. Shiren, by the way, was asleep.

Third period, history.

The mood of this class was a little different from the others. "All right, let's get started. Today we're learning about Sacred Blood cultural history," the teacher said, placing a traditional *kamishibai* picture-story show on the podium. The opening image read *A Simple Sacred Blood History*.

"Okay, here we go."

The first picture was of villagers smiling happily in the style of a fairy tale.

"Long, long ago, the Sacred Blooded lived peacefully, drinking blood throughout the world. It was a wonderful age where they all lived great lives IRL, as it were. But..."

The second picture showed a creature that looked like a red ogre whacking people with metal rods.

"But the foolish humans got pissed at the Sacred Blooded for their happy normie lives and started oppressing them. They said they couldn't be friends with us because we drank blood, so they persecuted us. And so they say that all the Sacred Blooded in Europe were eradicated, and they slowly vanished from all other regions throughout the world. In the tenth century, the humans secretly created a global extermination organization called the Virginal Father to start destroying the Sacred Blooded across borders. And our ancestors still survived by living their lives, pretending to be foolish humans."

Ryouta could hear some of the people in the class saying, "Humans really are the worst."

They probably were living as humans just half a year ago, though, so this wasn't the time for him to be making any witty rebuttals.

Additionally, they sometimes used the word *human* and all related words to include both Sacred Blooded and the literal human species—everyone besides themselves.

Ryouta felt uneasy on the inside. He'd done a quick search online last night and found that there was already plenty of publicly available information on the Sacred Blood Empire, and the oppression by humans was apparently true. Humans had worked to erase the Sacred Blooded from the history books over a thousand years ago. He even read that their previous emperor had also been killed.

But why were they talking about this in class now? Any of the Sacred Blooded should already know this, and if they were going to learn it at school, this should have been one of the first lessons.

Was this just antihuman propaganda that they were teaching throughout the year? If it was, then this could pose a serious problem for the human Ryouta.

"However..."

The third picture was a beautiful young woman. Beside it was *The Emperor*.

"On April sixth of this year—the sixth day in the Month of New Life, that is—our emperor overcame her grief at the assassination of her father, the previous emperor, and then she gathered all the Sacred Blooded from throughout Japan here in the old city of Akinomiya, caused a revolution, and created the country of the Sacred Blood Empire. Let us work hard so that our country may live on in posterity. Oh, and the name of the illustrator will be on the test."

"*That's* what you're putting on the test?!" Ryouta couldn't help but speak up.

"You're always supposed to know the illustrator's name in cultural history class."

"That's your point?! Oh, hey, Shiren, you're up."

Shiren was finally awake.

"You must've been worried when you heard about class, but there's no need." Shiren patted Ryouta's shoulder in an overfamiliar way. "Those are the images of artist Bluh D. Dee. The facial expressions are a dead giveaway. Bluh Dee developed a new genre called *kamishibai* fanart. I'll help you review once we get home."

"Still not important enough to learn about in school! And that's not what I'm worried about, okay?!"

"The biggest strength of *kamishibai* fanart is that it's created on the assumption that it will be exhibited. Many people have seen Bluh Dee's art, and so he's apparently gained quite a lot of work. You could call his plan a success."

"Could you stop saying *bloody* like it's a name?"

"And don't worry. The Sacred Blooded aren't going around saying silly things like *Kill the humans*. No one will gain anything from that, and it's not realistically possible, either. Her Eminence was originally planning on letting bygones be bygones."

From what Ryouta had seen in the English textbook, the Emperor had sounded like an odd duck, but at least she was understanding.

"There's a passage about the Emperor on the previous page, by the way."

Ryouta flipped through the pages of the history textbook. "Lemme see—'After the Emperor's first name comes her second name, Elisabeta, followed by her third name, Alexandra, followed by her names Floretina Sylvia Rosanna. In short, her full official name is her first name plus Elisabeta Alexandra Florentina Sylvia Rosanna plus last name—' Yeah, your emperor's a weird one."

"You'll be in big trouble if you speak ill of the Emperor, so keep your mouth shut."

"'Additionally, the Emperor's full official name is so venerable that it is not included. Her face is so venerable that it is also not included. It is unfortunate, considering her beauty—' I'm pretty sure the Emperor's the unfortunate one here."

"Stop! Don't speak of Her Eminence in contempt! A minion's sins are his master's sins, too!"

He did feel bad for that, so he decided to stop with the insults.

Fourth period, music.

First, they had to sing the national anthem at the beginning of the class.

"Sacred Blood Empire National Anthem"
Flames bellow, blood bursts, oh, let everything burn
to the ground ♪
The sword glints, the spear pierces, the country of
light, the Emperor of the Sacred Blood Empire ♪

Again, they were singing praises to the Emperor, but the tune was easy to sing, almost like a pop song.

"When the anthem was first released, people were talking about how it lifted their spirits, and how it even felt like the opening to a story. Her Eminence has such wonderful taste."

"I'm slowly becoming immune to your national praise, Shiren, but you're right about this song being easy to sing."

"Right? It's also very popular with children."

"The chorus is super-easy."

"There were talks of the Emperor creating a promo video where she transforms."

"Wait... Popular with kids? Transforming..."

The tune did sound like something he might have heard somewhere before...on Sunday mornings.

"Hey, aren't the melody for the chorus and the words just a straight-up copy of the theme song from *Fish Pier Squad Seafoosiers*? It's practically a parody!"

The original lyrics went something like *Taking the bait, harpoon pierces, oh, let's fish it all up. Sea urchin melts, crab innards roar, the men of the sea, Fish Pier Squad Seafoosiers.*

"And the textbook tells me the Emperor wrote both the music and the lyrics! No way that's legal! Come on!"

But Shiren remained silent. She was obviously listening; she was just ignoring him.

"Hey, say something. Wha...?"

He finally realized all his classmates were giving him worried looks.

"Ryouta, you'll get arrested if the police hear you say that... That's not something you should ever talk about... Suspicion that it's plagiarized is an open secret..."

"Does the Emperor have no pride...?"

"I keep telling you to stop dissing the Emperor! It's too risky!"

The next song, "Ah, Our Emperor of the Sacred Blood Empire," was another cover of a song from a very famous anime.

*Due to various reasons, the lyrics have been omitted.

"This is…another cover of an anime song."

"Mm. It's a cover of an anime theme song about a robot from the future and a clumsy boy and their friends—the brawny son of a shopkeeper, a boy with spiky hair who's the son of a company president, and a girl who takes three baths a day and takes violin lessons but is horrible at it and loves sweet potatoes but hides it and has a pet canary and is related to an art critic—and their adventures together."

"Why did you describe the last one in so much detail? And what about the rights for it?"

"Her Majesty said it's not a problem since we don't have diplomatic relations with Japan."

"Is she just a hack?!"

And so the very exciting (to Ryouta the human) series of morning classes came to an end.

Then came the much-awaited (especially to Shiren) lunchtime.

Ryouta went to the cafeteria, pulled along by his collar. He'd had no idea he'd be going to school today, so he hadn't made any lunch.

"By the way, Shiren, do you have a job or anything?"

Business was booming in the cafeteria, so the two took their places at the end of the line. It wouldn't be their turn for a while.

"Ryouta, a student's job is to concentrate on her studies. We are not permitted to take part-time jobs at maid cafés or anything of the sort."

"No, I didn't mean it like that. And why did you say maid cafés as your example?"

"There are currently thirty within the Empire."

That didn't seem sustainable considering the population ratio; ten or so would probably go out of business before long.

"Basically, I'm asking if you have enough money to just use the cafeteria without really thinking about it."

He'd been wondering, but it wasn't an easy question to ask.

"I get an annual pension of two and a half million sacred yen. It's plenty for me, so long as I don't make any lavish purchases."

"Pension? Oh yeah, your parents— Nah, never mind."

He had a bad feeling about suddenly broaching the topic of her family problems, so he stopped.

"This is a one-thousand-sacred-yen note, in case you were interested." Shiren handed Ryouta a bill.

"Considering what I've seen so far, I'm guessing I'm going to see the Emperor's face drawn on it? Wait, you're not supposed to show her face, right? Then what'll—?"

Immediately next to Hideyo Noguchi's face on the regular old thousand-yen note, it said "SACRED YEN."

In marker. By hand.

"This is clearly a Japanese thousand-yen note."

"No, it's sacred yen. The workers at the Imperial Mint write 'SACRED YEN' on each and every note. Right now, the Empire's economy is running well without any extreme deflation or inflation due to the hard work of the people. As we are an independent country, we are obviously circulating a currency that's different from Japan's."

Shiren had her chest puffed out. She sounded proud.

Not that there's much chest for her to puff out, Ryouta thought.

"Also, counterfeiting can land you a prison sentence of up to ten years or a donation of four hundred milliliters."

"A blood donation is punishment for the Sacred Blooded, huh…?"

"That's right. The Sacred Blooded are special because we drink blood. There is nothing more insulting than having your blood taken. If you see anyone in Japan giving donation trucks nasty looks, there's a ninety percent chance they're Sacred Blooded."

"You guys sure are a pain. Oh, hey, it's our turn."

As they chatted, they finally reached the front of the line.

Ryouta decided to order a reasonably priced udon of 250 sacred yen, since he had no money of his own.

Shiren ordered the most expensive thing on the menu, the Sacred Blood lunch, for 520 sacred yen.

He was a little irritated that she chose something so much more expensive than he did. Still, it wasn't his money.

"Hey, there's two seats open over there." She pointed to a dimly lit table far in the back corner.

"Why'd you pick the corner out of all these tables? Isn't that just going to make us feel—?" Just as he started asking his question, Ryouta noticed something.

There were a lot of gazes focused on him.

Most of the students were looking at him oddly, and a portion of the jealous looks came from the boys.

Sure, it was probably stressful seeing an unfamiliar student next to his apparent girlfriend (?). Of course people would get pissed if someone so brazen showed up out of the blue; that much was inevitable.

He could handle it, especially since it wasn't like anyone was going to suddenly punch him.

But when he heard what the girls were saying when they passed by, he realized he actually couldn't.

"That boy looks delish."

Th-they're definitely talking about me like I'm a snack...

And so Ryouta sat at the corner table. "All right, time to eat. Hey, this is better than I thought."

The red miso–style soup and the firm udon noodles went well together, almost too well for a school cafeteria. It was way better than what they had at his old school.

"Exactly. The Emperor's goal is to create a country satisfied with food, clothing, and shelter. It might just be the school cafeteria, but she wants more than to keep us from starving. She wants to fulfill the four pillars: *Fast! Cheap! Delicious! And you can collect points!* Otherwise, it can't operate as a business."

"The more I hear about her, the less great the Emperor seems."

"See, look, every twenty points you get a discou— Oh, I was so busy talking with you I forgot to show them my point card..."

Shiren's face had gone pale. A card with seven collected points on it fell onto the table.

"I forgot because I was talking to you. I should've been able to get two points today... This is all your fault..."

"Hey, come on! Don't blame your own mistakes on my existence!"

"Ryouta, you're in charge of my cards from now on. I'm going to Fresh-mart Warakia after school, so make sure you show the membership card. Members get twenty percent off on some products."

"The Sacred Blooded don't have much of a culture, do they? But still, this udon is really good. It's a little spicy, but I think I'll finish the broth." You could put anything into a rich seafood-based broth, and it would be good. "Wait, but this dark-reddish soup isn't…blood, is it?"

The idea frightened Ryouta, so he checked with Shiren just in case. He'd already had more than half of it, though.

"Oh, this mincemeat *katsu* is so crispy! This is the royal straight flush of flavors!"

"You don't need to talk like you're on TV. Listen, this isn't human blood, is it?"

"……Hey, you ever wonder who *really* masterminded the Honno-ji Incident and took down Nobunaga Oda?" She was clearly avoiding the topic.

"I think I'm gonna go to the bathroom…"

"Oh, I was joking. It's not blood; it's not. It's just regular red-miso soup! Blood is a particularly expensive ingredient, so we don't use it with school lunch!"

"Well, that's a relief. Then I guess we're fi— Wait, so you *do* use it in expensive meals?!"

Ryouta decided he wouldn't be visiting any expensive restaurants.

Shiren had already polished off her food. She ate quite a lot for being so small, as always. "Hmm. Your homemade meals are nice, Ryouta, but a simple cafeteria lunch is also delightful."

"Yeah, the student cafeteria here is good. So what were our classes in the afternoon?"

Shiren seemed somewhat uncomfortable at that.

"What is it? You look like a guy who accidentally got on the women-only car on a train."

"It's because *you* keep saying weird things… Idiot…"

Twenty minutes later, Ryouta realized what she meant by that.

*   *   *

The next class was health and physical education.

"It's just class, so I don't have to pay attention...but it's still embarrassing..."

Health and physical education meant learning about how the body was built, and Ryouta had never really gotten used to the topic in his own school, either. He was not thrilled about this class. And on top of that...

"Okay, we're starting on this page today. Can you see, Ryouta?"

Shiren slid her textbook over to Ryouta across their connected desks.

He'd received textbooks for Japanese, math, English, and all the basic subjects, but he ended up sharing a text with Shiren for less frequent classes, like health and PE.

Sharing this textbook with a girl almost felt like some kind of erotic humiliation.

This hour was apparently also special to the Sacred Blooded, so the boys in particular were behaving unnaturally.

"Okay, class. This is very important, so no need to feel embarrassed," the female teacher said, but that only made him more aware of the whole situation.

The title on the page in question read "Licking the Blood of the One You Love."

This was way more than he'd expected...

In the book, there was a photo of a man and a woman licking off the blood on each other's hands and feet.

"We Sacred Blooded greatly increase our own physical ability by licking the blood of the ones we love. We still don't understand the exact mechanics of it yet, but research confirms a secretion of a hormone related to motor capacity. However, considering how strong the effects are, licking a loved one's blood is counted as doping in marathons and other sports. As such, the practice is forbidden in those contexts."

Everything the teacher said went in one ear and straight out the other.

"Your face is bright red, Ryouta. I thought you were Japanese...," Shiren pointed out from beside him.

"Hey, this is a crazy fetish for Japanese people, too... And you're blushing just as much as I am."

Her face was so flushed, it almost looked as if she had a fever.

"I was afraid of people calling me Shiren the Bloodied Blossom."

"Can you not start acting like an edgelord out of the blue?" He was 100 percent sure no one was going to call her that. "Hey, do the Sacred Blooded think about licking the blood of the people they like?" He could only ask the question because he had no romantic feelings for her.

"Y-yeah. Both men and women think about it. Blood usually comes from open wounds. By putting a lot of your own saliva into the wound, it's just the same as making someone your minion…"

That was only if he were Sacred Blooded, though.

Biting Ouka, then licking her blood…then she'd do what he wanted…

Crap, he was getting excited! The thought of sucking Ouka's blood was too much of a turn-on!

As he dreamed of the impossible, Ryouta felt a bit of blood dripping from his nose.

Just as Shiren said during lunch, she took Ryouta to the grocery store once class was over.

He wanted Tamaki to show him around the library as one of the committee members, but it would be risky to ignore Shiren's orders.

They arrived about five minutes after leaving school. Like before, a new sign that read FRESHMART WARAKIA hung over what was originally a different grocery store.

"This is the closest supermarket to the Fuyukura household. There's a nice selection of produce here. It is called a Freshmart, after all. Shocked, aren't you?!"

"I don't think there's anything here for the Fuyukura household to brag about!"

The shop was a regular grocery store, with the fruit and vegetable sections right at the entrance. It appeared many of the customers were shopping in pairs, be they couples or otherwise.

"There are masters here shopping with their minions. I guess it's a common sight, though…"

Shiren's face was slightly red, and she was starting to shrink in on herself. She wasn't tugging as hard on the chain, either.

"These minions look less like their master's underlings, and m-more like their lovers…"

Suddenly thrust in front of a swarm of couples, Ryouta started feeling a little weird. *No way… The two of us probably look the same…*

"Oh, those two over there are definitely crossing the line. The grocery store isn't an amusement park! Get a room!" Embarrassed, Shiren tried to complain, but her voice betrayed her.

"Do you think these couples suck each other's blood like we saw in the health textbook…?"

It still hadn't been that long since class, so it was extra-fresh in their minds.

But wait, human couples probably did something similar, even high schoolers. He'd never really thought about it before.

"L-listen here, R-Ryouta. A master and minion must know their places as master and servant. This debauchery is honestly depraved. Don't you ever make this mistake… I-I'll never forgive you if you put your arm around me or whatever…"

"Obviously. I'd never do something like that…"

Shiren's expression was something halfway between relief and disappointment as she briefly took a deep breath— No, that's just what it looked like to him. *No way she would look disappointed! You're getting distracted!*

Ryouta silently gave himself a pep talk.

Concentrate on shopping. Become one with the shopping.

Shiren also appeared to have shaken off the previous mood. "I assign you as the head of cooking in our household, Ryouta. You will create superior dishes suited to my tastes!"

"Stop moving the goalposts like that. But I guess you might put blood in the food if I left it to you."

She handed him a shopping basket, and Ryouta began placing vegetables in it. It irritated him, being ordered around like this, but he didn't mind being in charge of cooking.

"These cabbages are pretty cheap. I could put together twice-cooked pork with some mushrooms. Do you have oyster sauce at home?"

"Ooh! You don't sound like a high schooler! I bet you were actually the

star of your home ec club, weren't you?" Shiren's eyes glittered. She probably wasn't eating very well, generally.

"I wasn't in the home ec club or anything, but growing up, I didn't really
have a choice but to cook for myself."

"Growing up...? Did you not have a mother...?" Shiren's expression
clouded over.

"Nah, it's nothing that tragic. She's alive and well."

"Then, like, was she your stepmother and never made you any food
because she was bullying you?"

"Why do you want to destroy my home life so bad?! I mean, you already
have, in a way! And my mom's food is really good, just so you know. A Chi-
nese person would eat it and yell *Haochi!*"

"Then it doesn't sound like you had older brothers or sisters who you
weren't actually related to and didn't let you eat because they hated you."

"I'm telling you, it was nothing like that! It was my sister! She had a
major obsession with me and brought me cake every day even though I
never asked for it! I'd eat the cream puffs she got for me without a care in
the world, until later when I found out they were from a real famous shop
that she lined up for before it even opened. The more I learned about what
she brought me, the harder it was to eat them!"

"Okay, then I can't think of anything else. Why?"

"My mom puts things in the food that shouldn't be there."

"Like trash?"

"I'm telling you, quit with the bullying. There's always a good chance the
food's drugged. Like with aphrodisiacs and stuff."

Shiren looked confused.

He really didn't want to explain, but he had no choice but to do it. "I
told you before—human girls get way too into me... And my own birth
mother isn't an exception. I think the first time was in sixth grade—I suddenly got really sleepy while I was eating, and I fell unconscious and ended
up locked in a confine—I mean, my room..."

"You were just going to say *confinement room*, weren't you?! What kind of
house did you live in?!"

"The way I grew up, the only food I could safely eat was stuff I made myself... And I wanted it to be good, so I practiced."

His hapless fate had given him a skill that proved to be useful in this situation—life sure had a funny way of working things out.

"Right, where are your parents, Shiren? They didn't seem like they were at home."

The topic of parents was a tricky subject, but she'd asked him first, so he was free to ask her without any guilt.

"Oh, Ryouta..." Shiren's expression changed. Had he crossed a line? What if they were deceased?!

"S-sorry. I didn't mean to offend you..."

"You move too fast, Ryouta... It hasn't even been twenty-four hours since we met. And we're only master and minion, at most..."

"I'm really sorry for hurting your fee— Huh?"

Shiren's cheeks were as red as a prized apple, exactly how she'd been when they saw the couples upon entering the store. Probably even redder. "Don't tell me you want to meet my parents already...? Do you really want to marry me that badly...? I am proud to say I'm higher than number two on the cute rankings at school, but... Let me just reiterate that I'm nothing more than your master. Think of it as a love across impassable social boundaries and just give up! B-but it's not like I hate you or anything, okay?!"

"Time out, time out! You misunderstood me! This is a mistake! And you don't have to brag about being the cutest girl in school in such a round-about way!"

"Even minions can legally become nobility... But if that happens, it's not like I won't—"

"Okay, enough! We're shopping! First, we've got our cabbage here."

Akinomiya had always produced cabbages, so they were cheap. Many of their own vegetables were locally grown. He quickly placed one into the basket.

"Put some tomatoes in next."

"Oh, the shiitake mushrooms are cheap. I can use this tomorrow."

"And tomatoes."

"Peppers are great, too. Maybe I could make some pepper steak."

"And you need tomatoes."

"We could use bananas for breakfast, so I'll get a bunch of those."

"We could also use tomatoes for breakfast."

"How many tomatoes are you putting in?! I look away for two seconds, and my basket is full of tomatoes!"

Seven tomatoes had popped into existence among the other vegetables.

"Tomatoes are a staple of the Sacred Blood diet. Tomato farmer Kenichi Takashima says, 'A tomato a day keeps the doctor away'!"

"Your source is a stakeholder in the industry, so that's not very convincing! And wait, are you telling me the Sacred Blooded are okay with tomatoes in place of blood? They're just the same color!"

"H-how rude of you! We don't place that much importance on superficial similarities! It's all about the flavor!"

"Do you like red or green peppers better?"

"Red peppers."

"You *do* care more about looks! Peppers might be different colors, but they taste the same!"

"What a despicable thing for a cook to say. Unlike green peppers, red ones are slightly sweeter."

"Okay, Master Chef, then why don't you cook it instead? We're moving on!"

And so they finished their business in the produce section. Beyond it was the section for fish and meat.

"Fish, hmm. We'll be having more meat for a little while, so we'll skip that. Hey, what's that over there?"

Next to the meat section was a row of clear bags filled with red.

"I haven't seen an ingredient like this before. What do we have—? *Blech.*"

When Ryouta approached and saw what the product was called, he couldn't even finish the sentence.

HUMAN BLOOD TYPE A: 200 ML—683 SACRED YEN

YOUNG HUMAN BLOOD TYPE B: 200 ML—1286 SACRED YEN

HUMAN BLOOD TYPE O: 200 ML—1488 SACRED YEN

HUMAN BLOOD TYPE A (TOKYO UNIVERSITY GRADUATE,
    YOUNG BUSINESSMAN, ¥60 MIL SALARY, PHOTO INCLUDED):
    200 ML—2471 SACRED YEN

"I thought so…"

"Let me dispel any misgivings you might have—the Sacred Blooded don't attack unsuspecting humans or anything like that. We send out fake blood donation trucks and collect blood that way. The trucks are terrifying, but on the flip side, it's a way for us to secure our precious blood. Plus, blood is an indulgence if anything. We don't have it as often as Japanese people have pork or beef, so there's no need for you to worry."

"How much blood given out of goodwill has disappeared into people's food…?"

Ryouta turned his gaze to the snack section to distract himself from his crawling skin and saw some tasty-looking potato chips, although they were from a brand he'd never heard of.

Now with human blood for a limited time!! it declared in large letters on the front, like a normal bag would advertise 20 percent more volume.

"I can't put blood into my food…"

"Fine. I'll compromise with that."

The sun had already long set by the time they finished shopping.

"Ooh, a sunset red as fresh blood!"

"Can you use a metaphor that sounds more like something a high school girl would say? Is this normal for the Sacred Blooded?"

"Well, what do you think, Ryouta? Have you gotten a sense of what it's like here in the Great and Grand Empire of Sacred Blood?"

"I learned that Sacred Blooded are pretty much the same as us."

After a full day, that was the conclusion Ryouta had come to.

Unsurprising, since the country had been made by people who had been living in the guise of humans (and probably over half as Japanese humans, specifically).

"I honestly thought Akinomiya would have had more of a demonic makeover, so I'm relieved."

Akinomiya historically had many valuable cultural assets, the most notable of which was the Akinomiya Shrine that had given the city its name. The main and worship halls had been built in the Muromachi period and were current national treasures.

"We only ever act in moderation, of course. People who buy too many 'grown-up' things are treated as children; our culture values temperance."

"By the way, aren't we a little too far from the road home?"

They weren't going the opposite direction, but they were rather off track.

"Mm. To end our day, I was thinking of showing you one of the cores of Sacred Blooded culture that makes us who we are."

"What do you mean?"

"Well, you seem to have the opinion that the Sacred Blooded and the Japanese are the same. There are many ways to characterize a people, Ryouta. Language, traditional practices, and what else?"

"Uh, I guess the gods they believe in, so…religion?"

"Yes, that's right. The Sacred Blooded have a faith called the Holy Church of the Sacred Blood. And the greatest cathedral with the greatest authority is just beyond here."

"Huh, I didn't know something like that was around here… Wait."

He had a sinking feeling.

Now that he thought back on it, both the school and grocery store had been repurposed to something similar to the original establishments.

And the road they were on was the approach to Akinomiya Shrine. A large torii gate towered right above Ryouta's head.

"See, Ryouta, this is the First Cathedral! Be sure to make plenty of offerings!"

No, it couldn't be…

The cypress-thatched, gabled roof of the magnificent, three-bay-wide main hall now had a gothic-style spire, and a new garish pink annex was sitting next to the temple itself.

A sign that read FIRST CATHEDRAL sat square in the middle of the torii.

"Ahhhhh! The shrine! An officially designated national treasure!! Did it get a demonic makeover?!"

"It's a beautiful sight, making a building so old into something new. Inside is the archbishop, Alfoncina the Thirteenth, who holds the greatest authority in our country's religious world. A mere minion like you typically wouldn't be able to meet her, but we are acquainted, so I'll make an exception to introduce you. You should be glad for your master's compassion."

Alfoncina XIII—now that was a majestic name.

Would she be wearing robes with a big crown on her head like a Roman pope? Would she whisper, *Repent!*? An image of Alfoncina XIII rose to his mind's eye.

"Why do you know someone so important anyway?"

Shiren ignored Ryouta's simple question, and—

Kalang-clang-clang! Kalang-clang-clang!

—rang the shrine bell with wild abandon.

"That's odd; I'm ringing the call bell, but she's not coming."

"Hey, I'm pretty sure that's not supposed to be a call bell. Are you sure it's okay you can call her so rudely like that? We're not gonna be thrown into jail for disrespecting a sacred place, are we?"

They were here to see an archbishop, so Ryouta was on edge.

It was no big deal if she was rude to her minion, but it would be bad for them if she forgot herself in front of someone with power.

"Hmm, she's not coming out at all. She can't be away, either. What is the meaning of this?!" Shiren was beginning to get irritated, and she started ringing the bell with even more vigor.

"Calm down!

"You have your wallet with you, right, Ryouta? Give me a hundred ye… sacred yen."

"You can just call it a hundred yen." Ryouta did as he was told and pulled out a one-hundred-yen coin.

"How do you like this, Archbishop?!"

Shiren held the coin high above her head.

Ting.

She threw it into the donation box.

At that moment, the door to the shrine opened. "Thank you for your donation! I am the (eighteen-year-old) archbishop! How may I be of service today?"

The woman who emerged was wearing a haphazardly arranged priestess uniform. Instead of a traditionally red *hakama* covering her legs, hers were all black.

"So you only come out when someone puts money in the donation box, Archbishop? You've added a whole new meaning to the phrase 'cash on arrival.'"

"Well, we can't build any more annexes to the cathedral without money, can we? Oh, I don't believe we've met. Hello!"

"Oh, I apologize on behalf of this rude idiot, Archbishop Alfoncina the Thirteenth!"

Ryouta hurriedly lowered his head and prostrated himself. He grabbed Shiren's head to pull her down with him. He heard her complaining ("Hey, what are you doing to your master?!"), but even a minion had to obey the higher authority.

"Ha-ha-ha, there's no need to humble yourself like that. Come in, come in. It's a little untidy, though."

The archbishop seemed unbothered as she went inside the shrine.

Ryouta was relieved she didn't seem to be too aware of the social hierarchy.

They entered the shrine and found cushions ready for them to sit on. A woman and an elder wearing black *hakama* immediately appeared from a side hallway with what Ryouta chose to believe was juice. They placed the cups down, then left.

"Those were the archbishop's minions. Once you reach her status, you get to have more than a dozen minions," Shiren leaned over to explain.

"Hmm, I don't know if they're my minions—more like my staff? We need plenty of hands to keep the cathedral running."

Ryouta looked at the archbishop once again. She had an abundance of hair ornaments—probably religious items—and she wore some kind of animal skull around her neck. The skull had an African feel to it, but her clothes were traditional Japanese. The combination was unnerving.

But still—she was cute.

Her light-pink hair and large greenish eyes brimming with curiosity really reminded him of a girl from a fantasy RPG. And unlike Shiren, she had an alluring maturity about her, despite how they were supposed to be only a year apart.

What he wanted to say was that this was the first time around here he'd met an attractive woman who was also mature.

There's no way she's more beautiful than Ouka... But I guess Shijou was cute, too—the Empire is incredible. Are these their genes?

"You're staring at the archbishop, Ryouta."

Ryouta felt a little awkward when Shiren pointed out the intensity of his gaze.

"Ha-ha-ha, boys sure are honest, aren't they? By the way, Shiren, who is he? He's not your boyfriend, is he?"

"He's my minion." "I'm her minion."

For the first time, Shiren and Ryouta were on the same page. He was ashamed calling himself a minion, though.

"His name is Ryouta. I found him yesterday. He still has some growing to do, but I will turn him into a minion with fantastic service, who will take care of the sore spots, who will be open twenty-four hours, who will work to be the cheapest of all Sacred Blooded and provide free tech support for a five-year period!"

"I'm not a big-box electronic retail store!"

But the archbishop wasted no time taking a crack at her.

"Your minion, hmm? But he clearly smells like a regular human."

"I'm… I'm still too young, so my blood power wasn't strong enough yet!"

"Hmm. Then are you going to bite this Ryouta every day to make him your minion? How adorable."

The archbishop looked at the two of them with a somewhat sly smile. Ryouta spat out his juice.

"Not if I have anything to say about it! It would hurt way too much for her to bite me every day, so no thank you!"

"Awww. Then why don't you bite Shiren as well? That way, you'll both be even."

It wasn't just the air around her that was so adult—even the way she talked was mature. Ryouta wanted to crawl into a hole…

"I-I'm going for a walk! You teach Ryouta about the church or whatever!"

Shiren left, probably because of the awkwardness. She'd even left the chain attached to his collar. If he tried to follow her, it would jingle.

"Hey! You're being irresponsible!"

And so, he ended up one-on-one with the archbishop.

Ryouta had never really dealt with situations like this very well; in the past, he'd been in a similar position, and someone had made advances on him. Being alone with women had become traumatic for him.

"Oh my, it's just the two of us."

The archbishop was staring hard at him. She must see him as a little brother. Yeah.

"Er, uh, yes, you're right…"

"Why did you go to school in the girls' uniform? Are you into that? Or is Shiren?"

"I don't have my own, so… Wait, why do you know that?!"

"Oh, the reason is simple. This might be a little too sexy."

The archbishop suddenly stood, undid her sash, and boldly threw off her priestess clothes.

"Whoa! What are you doing?!"

Ryouta instinctively turned his gaze downward, but the clothes she'd removed fell into his field of vision. This was too much!

"You can look, silly. I'm not wearing what you're expecting," she told him, perfectly carefree.

It was okay if she was right, but…her clothes were in a heap on the floor… But if she said it was okay, then she shouldn't mind. Right, okay. He wasn't at fault here!

Ryouta steeled himself and lifted his gaze only to see the archbishop wearing a gym uniform.

"Ta-daa! It's me, Alfoncina, from Year Three, Class Two. I'm an upper-classman at your school."

"Oh, right, eighteen is still high school age, isn't it? But is the archbishop allowed to be a high schooler? Pardon my disrespect, but I thought it was a job for someone with more experience…"

"Why not? I saw someone online say *Everyone after elementary school is old* before."

"I mean, that opinion is kinda biased, but sure, you could use it… Wait, you're right; it was online…"

He felt as if he'd seen an article online that said something like "Here Comes the Young and Beautiful Archbishop!"

"A high school archbishop draws attention, doesn't it? It's perfect for advertising, since the Emperor isn't allowed to show her face. And so, I think we'll be seeing a lot of each other at school from here on out!"

It made more sense when she explained it. It sounded as though it was all carefully planned out.

"Well then, little Ryouta, I'll show you around the cathedral! Follow me!"

The archbishop put her priestess clothes back on and smiled brightly.

"Ha-ha-ha-ha-ha-ha-ha-ha-ha-ha-ha!"

As they discussed how Ryouta came to find himself in the Empire, the archbishop burst out laughing.

She could hardly believe any of it—both how he was cursed to have women follow him everywhere and how he didn't know a thing about the Empire.

"Wow, it really does take all kinds. Now you'll have to live here in the Empire despite your ignorance, so be sure to learn about the Holy Church."

The archbishop explained to him as she guided him around the shrine.

"At first, the Holy Church of the Sacred Blood was not a well-defined faith, and we didn't have any organization like this. I think it was only first properly established about five hundred years ago. Those people from long ago believed we needed something to help us retain our sense of self as a people, and that we should have a real religion to accomplish that."

"I see. I've only just arrived here, so this is very informative."

Her outspoken nature was a relief to Ryouta, since he was still getting to know her.

But damn, she's hot. This should be illegal…

She was called the beautiful young archbishop, and if she ever decided she wanted to be an idol, she had the face for it. She was proportioned well enough to be in pinups, and she had to be at least an E cup.

"All right, next we'll be going into this room. Please watch out for the step there."

The archbishop took Ryouta's hand and showed him around what used to be the shrine. If they had been in town, it would have been like going on a date with an older student he'd always looked up to.

Even Ryouta, who thought he had chosen Ouka, felt a little flustered.

"Man, I sure wish someone like you had found me instead of Shiren."

Shiren herself wasn't around, so he felt free to joke at her expense.

"Really now?"

The archbishop froze in place in the middle of the hallway. Had he made her mad since he had insulted her friend?

"Well, I mean, not that it would ever happen even if I did mean it, so…"

"Now that I've explained most of the Holy Church of the Sacred Blood to you, let me hear more about you, Ryouta. Who are you? How did you come to the Empire?"

She was still smiling, but it was an odd question.

"Wait, I thought I just told you about that."

"So you like hiking in your free time, and you didn't know that Akinomiya had become Empire territory. You left your country and came into the city where you happened upon Shiren, who took you in since you had nowhere to go? Dear me, that won't do at all." There was something odd about the way she was acting. "That's much too suspicious to be a lie."

The archbishop whirled around to face Ryouta, but she wasn't smiling.

"After the Emperor, I'm the second most likely target for assassination. You need to be a little sneakier about it. The Virginal Father sure have been faltering lately, haven't they?"

Her eyes were filled with enough hate to kill a bunny or hamster, or so it looked to him.

And yet, her mouth was spreading wide in a grin.

"This really is a misunderstanding! I'm not…"

"There were quite a few in the past—people who wanted to kill me and take back Japan's dignity. And it was so obvious that they were clearly just after my body. Doesn't that make you laugh? I had them killed, of course."

The air around them had turned bloodthirsty, nothing like before. She would kill him at this rate.

"You're making a mistake! I'll explain at school tomorrow!"

Throwing politeness to the wind, Ryouta dashed forward. He needed to get out of this building, and fast!

"I don't think you'll be able to leave the cathedral unharmed." He heard her icy voice behind him.

"Um, did we come this way? Crap! It's all redone, so it's like a maze now!"

He wanted to punch himself for thinking yesterday that he could live peacefully in this country, if even just for a brief second.

Considering his position, being mistaken for a spy wasn't out of the question.

No matter where he ran, there were minions—the archbishop's, of course. There was no time for him to admire the cathedral, either.

"I feel like I'm getting farther and farther from the exit…"

He then found himself in front of a room with a plaque that read Alfoncina's Room. It was probably a dead end in here, but he had no choice but to go inside.

"I can at least lock the door from the inside, right? …Uh."

Ryouta slipped inside and frantically locked the door—and then he fell speechless.

The room was buried in dolls.

Well, they weren't so much dolls as figurines of cute girls. Rows and rows of characters with pink and blue hair and glittering eyes.

"Why does she have so many figurines…?"

"So you saw." The archbishop entered behind him. She held a key in her hands. Apparently, she'd unlocked it from the outside. "Well? What do you think? The thirty-eight magnificent members of the Alfoncina Krafted Band caught you in their brilliant trap. I call them AKB38."

"Damn, you are plagiarizing like crazy just because we don't have any diplomatic relations!"

"So now that I've led you into the most important idol room of the temple, what do you think?"

"They're just figurines… And you've really messed up some of them; they're way more inappropriate now…"

He wasn't sure he could take having this room as his deathbed.

"Look there, farther in."

The archbishop was pointing to the bronze statue of a girl. Bat-like wings sprouted from her back.

It looked like Dracula flying through the sky—no, something about it seemed more divine, more holy.

He was cornered right now, yes, but Ryouta was enthralled by the statue in spite of himself. That was how overwhelmingly beautiful it was. He'd only ever experienced something like this in an art museum before.

"That is the Goddess of Blood, the deity of the Holy Church of Sacred Blood. The most important rituals take place before our god here in this room. For example, executions of evildoers."

"Crap! I've got better things to do right now!"

There were no windows in this room.

"Well then, I think my little trick should start taking effect just about now."

Ryouta's body was suddenly sapped of strength, and he collapsed.

"I had a little poison mixed in with your juice. There's no serious threat to your life, though."

If the situation were any different, the archbishop would've been wearing a sultry smile that could've made his heart skip a beat.

Everything had been part of her plan from the very start. Ryouta hated how he'd underestimated her.

"Are you going to kill me now…? But I guess it's all my own fault. I had no idea the next town over was a totally different country…"

"Oh, it's not your fault."

The archbishop cupped Ryouta's face with her hands.

If we were in a manga, she'd be about to take my neck and snap it in half…

There was no way he would get home alive if they thought he was a part of the Virginal Father, the secret society of humans who wanted to kill the Sacred Blooded. And he'd just learned about them in school today.

"Oh, what a lovely face you have. Look at the line of your nose and the shape of your eyes." Now she was toying with his face. He just wanted her to kill him and get it over with. "Your eyebrows are neat, like you take good care of them. Oh, you're perfect!"

If you're gonna do it, just do it!

"And look how *cute* you are when you're frightened. Why don't you try on my priestess clothes? I'm sure you would look great in them!"

At least she liked him, apparently.

"Uh… What about me being a spy or that you're going to kill me and stuff…?"

"Oh, that hardly matters!"

"Yes it does matter!"

Of all the things to disregard, that shouldn't have been one of them!

"You haven't noticed? I'll be honest—I tricked you."

Tricked...me... What she said registered in Ryouta's mind right away. "Wait, what do you mean...?"

"How about four hundred thousand a month?"

That was an oddly precise number. The archbishop slowly leaned closer and closer to Ryouta.

"How does four hundred thousand a month to be my minion sound? I might be just a high schooler, but I have quite the salary—so how about it? All you need to do is let me suck your blood..."

"Don't tell me you were treating me like a spy just to lead me in here?"

"My, I'm happy we finally have our own country, but that means all the humans are gone, and there's no way for me to get any fresh blood anymore. Then I thought about how oh-so-lucky I was that Shiren brought in my very type of Japanese boy. I think you're the only Japanese person in this entire country."

"I'm telling you, I'm Shiren's minion! Taking someone else's minion isn't ethically—"

"Legally, you are still just a plain human. And if I'm left with no choice but to bite a spy, then that still counts as self-defense, right? Well, anything untoward I'll just cover up with my power as archbishop."

He shivered. He felt the same fear as he did when his sister had assaulted him not too long ago.

"Oh, are you nervous? Don't tell me you—"

What she whispered in his ear knocked him for a loop.

"G-g-girls shouldn't say stuff like that! It's crude!"

The archbishop smiled pityingly at the flustered boy.

"Oh, so you are inexperienced. It seems like I won't be getting your approval, so I'll have to use force. I suppose I'll start with your right arm, then, hmm? First, antidote."

She extended her tongue and licked his arm. Out of context, it was pretty erotic.

His heart was beating like crazy, although this situation really didn't call for it.

He would be her minion at this rate. Even if minions weren't just plain slaves, and serving a master was an honorable profession, he still hated that this would decide the course of the rest of his life.

"Oh, you're quite salty. Have you been sweating? Oh, not that I'm complaining, of course."

The archbishop's tongue trailed up his arm as she spoke, and he felt more of her weight on him. Was that her chest pressing against him? And since she was wearing the priestess outfit, her chest was being exposed quicker than anything else.

I say exposed, *but all I can see is her gym outfit... Wait, why is this turning me on...? W-wait! I've heard of a priestess fetish, and I've heard of gym uniform fetish, but I've never heard of seeing-a-gym-uniform-through-the-priestess-robes fetish! Is that even a thing?! Is that too specific?!*

Ryouta tried to shake his head in protest—he wasn't that kind of pervert!—but his body wouldn't move. It was the drugs.

There was only one future he could see, and it would involve his blood getting sucked.

But he hadn't given up on hope yet.

His (eventual) master was somewhere in this shrine!

And as his master, Shiren Fuyukura was obligated to save him—probably!

She had apparently gone to walk the grounds, but she'd come back inside the hall once she noticed the commotion—probably!

If they followed the rules of anime and manga—no, the universal rules of drama—then the hero would come in as he reached the line between life and death and save him—probably!

"All right then, it's time for me to have some of your blood now, I suppose. Ohhh, how long has it been since I've had fresh human blood!"

I know this should be the other way around, but, Shiren, help me!

Chomp.

Alfoncina XIII dug her teeth into Ryouta Asagiri's right arm and started sucking his blood.

Wait, help wasn't coming for him???

Shiren wasn't here. She was probably lazily wandering around right about now.

Now that things had come to this, Ryouta really started panicking.

Am I going to have to lead a second life as Alfoncina the Thirteenth's minion…? Is that what the rules say…?

But he couldn't stand the idea.

The odd mixture of pain and euphoria quickly enveloped him.

Plainly speaking, it felt super-good! Really, super, incredibly good! His body was melting! Melting into fluff! Fluffy mush!

"Doesn't it feel good? Humans feel an overwhelming sense of euphoria when bitten by the Sacred Blooded. Plenty of gentlemen out there decided to become minions solely to experience this ecstasy."

He wasn't totally clueless as to why someone would do that. The feeling was addictive. *Wait, no, calm down.* He'd never get home at this rate!

"N-no, I already have someone in my heart I… O-Ouukkhha! Eee!"

He tried calling out for Ouka, but he couldn't.

"Ohhhha! Oukyya! Ahhh, no! C-crap! Ah! Gahhh! Hrrrrg!"

Ryouta clenched his teeth, somehow managing to keep his head and resist. From just his voice, it sounded as if he wasn't thinking, only feeling, but that wasn't the case at all. He could see the other side. And once he crossed over, there was no coming back.

Like savoring sweet candy, the archbishop slowly bit into him. She bit then licked, licked then bit, over and over again. It was almost as though she knew doing it this way would put Ryouta in the most blissful state she could manage.

"Does it feel that good? Then shall I try something on you that will make you feel even better once I completely make you my minion? …Oh dear, how embarrassing—never mind that one!"

Her teeth pierced his skin again. At the same time, her nails dug into his other arm. It was as though she was trying to control him with both sensuality and torment, and more and more of Ryouta became the archbishop's.

Ryouta was losing the energy to fight back. There was probably some sort of paralyzing effect that was activated by a bite from the Sacred Blooded.

"I think you should be my minion in about two minutes."

No, I can't think anything anymore. I'm almost done for...
Just when Ryouta was a bite away from giving in—

"What are you doing, Archbishop?! Ryouta is mine!!!"

—Shiren finally came back.
"Oh dear, I've been found out."
The archbishop briefly stood and folded her hands toward Ryouta in a gesture of apology.
Wait, that was it? She'd been biting him...
"Alfoncina the Thirteenth is notorious for being the naughtiest archbishop in history. She's also the one who set up the trap to drop a blackboard eraser and washtub on the Emperor during her coronation ceremony."
"Shouldn't she be executed for that?"
The archbishop giggled and scratched her head. Was this really the time...?
"And I forgot that she's the type to steal other people's minions with a straight face... I bet she made up some random reason to make you her minion, like you're a spy or something, didn't she?"
"Whoops, you got me!"
"I know everything that goes on in that lewd mind of yours, Archbishop! Heh." Shiren puffed out her nonexistent chest in pride, and Ryouta ever so slightly wanted to murder her.
"If you knew everything, then you should've come to save me in time... She already bit me."
Shiren's face went pale with shock.
"It's fiiine. I only bit him for a minute or so," the archbishop reassured them.
"O-okay... She can't make you her total minion without a serious bloodsucking. Looking at you, it seems like she was only really nibbling at you, so you'll be fine."
"Yes, only a nibble. You came back before I could get to the real biting."
Real biting? That sure felt like real biting to him.
"But it's clear he has the makings of a good minion. If you call him over with a very strong will, his minion power could pull him to you. Like, *Sorry! Can you return my rental DVD?*"

"Do I only exist so you can avoid paying late fees? Do people even still rent DVDs around here?"

"Anyway, you can't do this anymore, Archbishop. If I grow up to be important one day, I'm throwing you in jail. And then I'll call you by your real name for the rest of your life."

"N-no, anything but that!" The archbishop suddenly started bowing incessantly. She must really hate her name.

"What's her real name? Does she end up being cursed and controlled by whoever calls her by her true name or something?"

"Matsuko Kimura."

"Wow, that was unexpected. And plain. And boring."

"Stop it! 'Archbishop Matsuko Kimura' just isn't snappy! People will lose their faith! Just give me a break!"

"Then never, ever do anything like this again. Okay, Ryouta, you can stand now, can't you? Let's go."

Shiren grabbed Ryouta's hand and pulled him up.

Wait, she didn't pull my chain... Well, I guess this doesn't hurt as much, so it's fine with me.

Ryouta staggered as he stood up.

And her hand is weirdly warm... Nah, forget about it.

"Hmm? What is it, Ryouta?"

"...Uh, nothing."

Shiren's arms then wrapped around him, as if she were desperately trying to steady a large pillar.

"Huh?"

"You are my minion. Even if someone else tries to drink from you, you're still mine."

Shiren kept a tight grip on him, claiming her right over him.

Ryouta was a little happy, but at the end of the day, he was still sad. In this country, he was an object.

Even though he was no longer being targeted by every single woman, he was now seen as a *thing* that could be turned into a minion by every single Sacred Blooded. The archbishop was just one of many.

And so was Shiren...

"No one can replace Ryouta as my minion. Unlike you, Archbishop, I'm not okay with just anybody."

Shiren glared sternly at the archbishop. It was almost as though she was willing to face the consequences of disrespecting her.

What...? Am I not an object to Shiren?

"Fine. I won't try anything for a week."

The archbishop smiled bitterly, acknowledging Shiren's claim— *Wait, one week is really short! Is she going to try to bite me again in a week?!*

Shiren tugged at his hand. "We're going now."

"Right. Good-bye, Archbishop."

It was overall a terrible experience, but Ryouta respectfully bowed his head. She was still a person of authority.

"Buh-byeeee. Oh, Shiren, that's right. Your next inspection is soon."

"...Yeah, right." Shiren looked just a smidge unhappy to Ryouta.

Inspection? Who's coming for that?

"Got it?! You are not to let anyone but me bite you! Not even Her Majesty herself!"

Shiren yelled at him the whole way home, only she was angry like a girl who'd caught her partner cheating.

"I know. But she really knew what she was doing; I don't think I could have gotten out of it... But still, thank you..."

"Huh?" Shiren's expression went blank.

"You said I was irreplaceable. I could tell you would honestly treasure me as your minion, unlike the archbishop."

He had been thinking about running the moment he got his chance, but it might not be all terrible to stick around with Shiren, he thought.

Not expecting the gratitude, Shiren froze. "Wha—?! O-obviously, this is exactly what a master...is supposed to do! I'm... I'm glad to see you've finally recognized my greatness, Ryouta—"

"But I guess it could be fun serving the archbishop. Still, she goes to the same school as us, so maybe I can just call her Alfoncina. I mean, she's gorgeous."

"Oh-ho. Is that a challenge, Ryouta? I'll bend you if you say that again."

Shiren bent a finger in a direction it was not meant to bend.

Ryouta's finger, to be precise.

"Owwwwwwwwwwwwwwowowowowow! You're not bending anything, you're *breaking* it! Stop!"

"Hmph! I was a fool to have believed you! You will make the most delicious dinner for me once we get home! At least serve me as my minion!"

Then the text notification went off on Ryouta's phone.

In an effort to avoid getting homesick, he'd been making sure not to stop to look at his texts when they came in.

Even though he'd texted his family to let them know he couldn't come home, he hadn't sent anything to his classmates. He was probably getting worried messages—

TITLE: To the Greatest Ryouta
MESSAGE: Dearest Ryouta, I am very, very, very, very, very worried about you, since you aren't able to come to school. If you can't come tomorrow, I will have to hole up in a temple and perform every incantation I know. How is life in Akinomiya? If possible, I would like to kill the vampire attached to your hip—beating, poisoning, punching, slicing, all of the above—but all forms of transportation in are cut off, so I can't enter the country. To think that while we were innocently living our lives, a vampire was suddenly attacking you in the shrine…! Please forgive me for being so powerless. I will take all the relatives of the vampire that tried to rape you, from her grandparents to grandchildren, and throw them into the crimson flames of hell. Every last one of them! I will soon be by your side!

Yours truly,
Kiyomizu Jouryuuji

It was unclear how she knew what was happening just a few moments ago.

He hadn't even mentioned he was in Akinomiya…

Ryouta vowed to double-check that the Fuyukura household wasn't bugged when they got home.

EPISODE 3
LET'S LEARN ABOUT THE GEOGRAPHY
OF THE SACRED BLOOD EMPIRE!

"In what was once the city of Akinomiya, over ten thousand residents have been taken as slaves called 'minions.' Despite not recognizing the Sacred Blood Empire as a sovereign country, the government is supplying them with copious rations each day with the intent of protecting our citizens. However, there is no doubt that this is only delaying the rescue of those imprisoned. Is it now time for our nation to take decisive measures?"

The image on the screen changed from a studio to show a Sacred Blooded house, indicated by the on-screen text.

All the faces in the house were blurred out. The voices were also distorted to add a layer of privacy.

A male minion was placing soup bowls before a whole family of Sacred Blooded in a very wealthy-looking dining room. For some reason, the man was wearing nothing but a pair of briefs.

"Today's soup is matsutake mushrooms in a clear broth."

"Let me see. Ugh, awful!"

The Sacred Blooded emptied the bowl onto the mostly naked minion. The man gave a cry and leaped back.

"You think I can have soup that tastes like sewage?! Call the landlady!"

Just as the minion started bowing his head, Shiren shut off the TV.

"Once it gets this bad, it's actually pretty entertaining."

That was a documentary from a Japanese public broadcast, called *Now in the Sacred Blood Empire*. However, the point seemed to be to insult the Sacred Blooded and their empire.

"That was staged, wasn't it?"

"Obviously. Where are you going to find an upstanding butler who only wears underwear? If word of a Sacred Blooded abusing their minion got out, it'd damage their reputation. Minions are treasure to us, not something to be treated so roughly— Ryouta, get the tea. I'll empty the whole pot on you if it's not hot enough."

"I'm noticing a bit of hypocrisy here!"

He poured out the hot water from the pot and placed it in front of Shiren.

"Phew, what a good meal. The mushroom-loaded curry you made today was delicious, Ryouta. I shall commend you. I'll gladly pay for you if you want to go to culinary school."

"You will? But you're just living on a pension—that wouldn't be enough to get you to college."

Ryouta looked with a tired expression at Shiren, who was lying down in the living room after dinner.

This was how it always was in the evening.

There wasn't anything particularly important for them to do, so they would spend their time lazing around after dinner. That was why they had been watching such a boring TV program.

It was Thursday. After school was finished the next day, it'd be Ryouta's first weekend.

I sure got used to this quickly…

He'd been living in the Empire for a few days now, but it wasn't much different from Japan.

It wasn't a hell where minions were doomed to a miserable fate, at least, but it wasn't exactly perfect.

The Sacred Blooded were serious about getting their own minions. Even if a butler was treated and paid properly, anyone would rather be the master than the butler. And if getting one was as easy as sucking some blood, of course they'd want one.

It was even the same in Ryouta and Shiren's class. Their classmates acted nice on the surface, but they were ready and willing to bite him if they had the chance.

The girls were especially polite and friendly with Ryouta. And by *friendly*, we mean on a dragging-him-into-the-gymnasium-storage-room level of friendly. And that had happened twice already. Almost every other day now.

©Hiroki Ozaki

It was basically the same as when he lived in Japan, possibly even worse. Once he was bitten, he'd be out for the count.

In this country, the only one who doesn't treat me like prey is…

Ryouta looked sadly at Shiren as she yawned on the couch.

"*Yaaawn.* I get so tired after eating. Wake me up in half an hour. I've heard that a thirty-minute nap is good for you, and I pay very close attention to my health."

As she yawned, her shirt lifted to expose her belly button. *Just get sick already*, he thought.

She's really the only one… Everyone else looks at me like a snack… It honestly feels like I'm living in a country full of assassins…

He hated to admit it, but Ryouta's only safe haven was here in the Fuyukura house.

It seemed as though she was really planning on falling asleep with her stomach exposed, so he threw a thin blanket over her.

"Ooh! This is just what I expected from the minion I picked out. How considerate of you!"

"A girl your age should have a little more modesty."

"There is no need for me to consider modesty before my own minion."

Shiren's attitude said, *What's so embarrassing about showing my stomach? It's not a big deal.*

Sure, her stomach wasn't exactly much of a turn-on. But if it were Tamaki or Alfoncina, that would be a different story.

"Hmm, y'know what this is like?"

"What is it, Ryouta?"

"Being an old married couple."

Ryouta thought it was a pretty good metaphor, himself. They weren't embarrassed around each other, despite being the opposite sex. She could sleep in his presence with her stomach exposed. This wasn't even boyfriend-girlfriend level; this was married-couple level. The way they were right now, one of them could start complaining about the smell of the other's socks without serious consequences.

In a way, this was the exact kind of relationship Ryouta was looking for.

Even if this was kind of an extreme case, it was a win if a man and a woman got this close.

Ryouta had spent his days in regular society being targeted over and over again, like a zebra being chased day in and day out by lions. It had made him wish for a calm space like this, more than anything else.

To him, this roommate situation was ideal.

I think I could manage as a minion for a long time.

And if the person who fell asleep beside him wasn't Shiren, but Ouka...

In his mind, Ryouta replayed everything Shiren had said, except that Shiren herself had been replaced by a seventeen-year-old Ouka.

"Ahhh, that was great. I guess the only thing you're really good at is cooking, Ryouta, but I suppose I'll praise you for that."

"C'mon, we're married. Why do you sound so condescending?"

"Well, you're the one who married me, and you seem pretty happy about it. Phew, I get so sleepy after dinner. Wake me up in half an hour."

"Hey, your stomach's showing. Be a little more modest, will you?"

"Does it matter? You've seen much more than my stomach."

It was way better than he had hoped.

He decided he would run this little simulation every day.

That was how things would probably be if he married Ouka—she might be a bit high-handed with him, but nothing extreme.

Could he trade Shiren in for Ouka?

But if he were with Ouka, then they'd probably act less like an old married couple and more like eternal newlyweds, but his relationship with Shiren now was more the former.

"Man, this whole mellow vibe really is a lot like being an old married couple. Not that I've ever been married, but..."

Now that his mind had slipped into a fantasy, he mentioned it aloud.

There was no romantic meaning to it at all, of course.

But when Shiren heard him say *married couple*, her reaction was way different.

"M... M-m-m-m-m-m-marrie—?!"

Shiren seemed oddly panicked, so much that she couldn't even say the word and cut herself off by biting her own tongue. She was flustered, everything to the tips of her ears bright red.

"Don't get ahead of yourself, Ryouta! We are master and servant! Our relationship is nothing like that of husband and wife or boyfriend and girl-friend! Even if we do become close, there are still lines I will not cross! Like Mito Komon and Kaku and Suke might really trust one another, right? But it's not like Suke would ever say *Hey, Komo, couldja pass me the remote?* Even if his life depended on it. You really need to have a good think about this!"

Shiren threw off her blanket and leaped up. Her drowsiness had van-ished in a flash.

"You don't need to get *that* angry. You're overreacting."

But his attitude only made Shiren even more indignant.

Her eyebrows turned down into a V, or like the arms in the \(^o^)/ face.

"Ryouta, did you *seriously* say 'We're like an old married couple' without thinking about the implications?"

"Well, yeah. Why? Did it make you think anything different?"

"Grrrr… I know it makes sense, but it still makes me mad. Why…?" Something inside Shiren snapped. "Oh, Ryouta, I'm hungry. Go buy me jam bread from the convenience store. Now."

"What?! I thought you were so full, you were falling asleep!"

"I burned calories being angry with my lousy minion. I'm going to starve. You can have the change and use it as your allowance. Here, take it."

A silver coin with a hole in the middle flew toward Ryouta.

By Japanese law, that would be a fifty-yen coin.

"I can't buy a piece of jam bread with fifty yen!"

"Who told you to buy *a* jam bread? Buy me three, *three*! And that is fifty *sacred* yen, thank you!"

Ryouta thought about how much she forgot when she got desperate.

"And what about this?" He pointed to the collar around his neck. "You're not coming with me. I might get eaten if I go out alone, remember?"

Shiren didn't even have to say *I totally forgot*. It was practically written in bold font on her face.

She hurriedly wrote something on a piece of cardboard.

"Okay, put this around your neck and go!"

It was a sign that said I AM THE MINION OF THE FUYUKURA FAMILY. It was even threaded with a string to put around his neck.

"You want me to put this on? Seriously?"

"Yes. Now you should have no problem."

"No."

"Get out! I tell you to leave, you leave! I don't want to see your face at all right now!" Shiren was practically screaming at him.

As for Ryouta, he was getting irritated himself. "What makes you think I want to see *your* face?!"

When he left the house, a cool breeze washed over him, calming him down for just a moment.

And here I was, thinking about how I could be a minion for a long time, but I guess I let my imagination run away with me...

It was only a five-minute walk to the store, but it was embarrassing enough for him.

He was walking around with a sign on his chest that read I AM THE MINION OF THE FUYUKURA FAMILY, after all. Like he was at a protest, although he had no idea what he'd be protesting.

"They were laughing at me... In the five minutes it took to get here, three people started snickering at me..."

Ryouta was still angry as he made his way to the store. Shiren became tyrannical like that sometimes. When she did, she always used her privilege as his master to do whatever the hell she wanted.

Just last night, she'd come to him with tears in her eyes and said, "There was a roach in my room! You stand guard next to my bed!" And he managed only four hours of sleep that night.

"If she gives me any other weird orders, I'm seriously leaving!"

As he walked, stewing in his irritation, he reached the convenience store.

It was called Nine-to-Eleven, which sounded like the name of a certain other company.

"So it opens at nine in the morning and closes at eleven at night? I don't think the office workers can use it in the morning, then. Is that okay?"

He commented on something that was almost entirely irrelevant, then went inside. He'd buy the stuff he needed, then go straight home.

Actually, he didn't really want to go back. He didn't want to see her.

"Welco— Oh, what a surprise, Ryouta!"

The familiar voice surprised him in turn.

"Oh, Tamaki...Shijou?"

He never expected to run into a classmate here.

Library committee member Tamaki was doing a lot to help him in class. Well, more like Shiren had no intention of helping Ryouta even though he'd just started at an unfamiliar school.

Tamaki was teaching him high school survival tips like "When that teacher writes words in yellow chalk, that means it will definitely be on the test" and "This teacher gets really angry when you sleep and hits you with the textbook."

She tended to think a little negatively, but that aside, she acted like a kind elder sister to him.

She actually had a lot of guys who liked her. Ryouta, being a guy himself, could tell right away.

She's practically a perfect superhuman, despite how tragic she is. She seems like an artsy type, but she's well put together. But, I guess, that aside...

"Part-time job?"

"No. My family runs this convenience store. It has such a bleak future, with terrible wages and nothing commendable about it. At night, delinquents will gather out front and make me anxious, and boys who are obviously in middle school come read *Eden of Pleasure*, even though the porno magazines are only for people eighteen-plus. Heh-heh."

"You don't need to be so negative about it."

As always, she was being excessively humble, but that was just Tamaki's natural setting.

"This spot is both our store and our living space. I live together with my mother and father—my fifth father and seventh mother, that is."

"Your family tree is way too complicated, Shijou!"

"So what have you come here for? I don't believe you're old enough to buy *Eden of Pleasure* yet."

"Is that the only reason I can come here?!"

"If you're not here to buy pornography, then…you're here to shoplift, aren't you…?"

"I can't believe that's how you think of high school boys…" He was rather shocked to learn that his only options were porn or theft.

"No, I was just thinking about how emotionally difficult it must be for you, since you came to the Empire all of a sudden. Now that a few days have passed, you should be beginning to wonder whether you'll ever adjust, whether you'll be able to keep up, your heart slowly breaking under the stress."

"…Bingo, Shijou. You're really sharp…"

She'd read him like an open book.

"Yes. Ever since I was a little girl, I've always had to have a good read on my parents, since we're not related."

"Wait, you can't just bring up heavy stuff like it's no big deal! Shijou!"

"Please come talk to me if you're ever in any trouble. I mean, if you're all right with someone like me, I'll do my best to help." Tamaki chuckled softly with an elegant smile. Shiren could never pull off that expression.

Ryouta was touched. *Shijou is such a great person…*

If I ended up married to Shijou, I feel like our home would be incredibly peaceful. It might be ordinary, but maybe that's the happiest place to be, in a way… Wait, what am I thinking?! I need bread.

He took three pieces of jam bread from the bread aisle and brought it to the register.

"So you're getting *three*…"

He knew she'd say something. It didn't exactly give a great impression.

"There's a reason for this."

"Are you Uncle Jam from *Anpanman*, Ryouta?"

"What? No, why did you think of that? He can make bread on his own."

"My only friends are love and courage and my ball, but I have two hundred fifty friends online."

"You're hinting that online friends aren't real friends, aren't you?"

"So why do you need that much jam bread…?" she asked. They were finally back on topic.

"Shiren is making me run errands. Just errands."

"I see; that's why you're wearing that sign on your chest. I thought you had some sort of public-shaming fetish."

The reminder of his appearance still gave him a nasty shock.

"But please do help her out so that Fuyukura can smile. She's been enjoying herself immensely since you came."

"Wait, she's not like that all the time? I can barely tell, since we live together." He had a feeling Shiren's personality never changed, even when he wasn't around.

"I knew I had to do something for her as well, but I never found a way to help. I could never manage what you're doing now." A serious expression briefly crossed Tamaki's face before she smiled again. "Please accept her as she is. And in exchange, I'll help you with your troubles," Tamaki said, almost sounding like Shiren's big sister.

"You're like an angel, Shijou. I wish you were the one who picked me up instead of her. I could live forever in a faraway land if I were with you."

"What do you mean...?" Tamaki stared back at him with a blank expression. Her hand holding the bread stopped midmotion.

"What? I mean exactly what I said." Unsure of what just happened, Ryouta gave a straightforward reply.

"I see... Very well. Okay, here is your jam bread. Um, that comes to..."

Then when Ryouta went to take the bread and pull out the money from his wallet—

Come here, come here, come here, a nice man will give you candy so come here, we want you to answer this survey so come here, come come come come come come come come come come come come come come come come

—the phrase *come here, come here* repeated in his head like an incantation.

"Whoa! What the hey?! What's this voice in my head?!" Barely able to keep himself still, Ryouta dashed through the store's automatic doors.

"What?! You haven't paid yet! Shoplifter! Are you stealing because this is my house?!"

"I'm sorry! My body's moving on its own!"

An endless loop of *come here* played in his mind. Nothing happened when he plugged his ears, since the words were coming directly in his brain. And his legs were moving on his own, carrying him somewhere.

He eventually found himself carried through the nighttime town and stopped in front of Akinomiya Shrine—rather, the First Cathedral.

"Oh, there he is." Alfoncina XIII stood in front of the grand cathedral.

"Wait, why did I end up here…? I ran all the way here without thinking about it…"

"I wanted you to come, so I called for you. For the record, I did bite you and sort of made you my minion. If I really concentrate, I can bring you to me. I've *so* been looking forward to this."

Alfoncina XIII looked hard at Ryouta with big, sultry eyes.

When he remembered what happened just a few days ago, he found himself getting anxious.

She had bitten into him hard that day. And so, even though he wasn't normally bound to anyone's will, if Alfoncina wanted to call him over, she could.

"Now that you mention it, Shiren did say you could at least call me over…"

Ryouta felt like his human rights were being infringed upon, and his heart sank.

"Awww, it's all right. I can't make complicated orders to a minion with little loyalty. This is the most I can get out of you, really. There's no danger to you at all, dear."

"So what do you want? You're holding a pot."

Alfoncina indeed held a big pot in her hands. "I made too much, so I'm sharing with you. I like to call this event I Have Some Food, Do You Want Some?"

"Usually, it's the person who made the food going around to offer it! And what did you make too much of?"

Ryouta was rather interested in what other people made, since cooking was one of his specialties.

"Oh, this is a very popular homemade dish. Tentacle—"

That was *not* a word he expected to hear when talking about homemade food.

"Oh, sorry, sorry! Slip of the tongue! It's *nikujaga*! Meat and potatoes, I promise!"

"Phew. If you were going to say that tentacles were a typical home dish for the Sacred Blooded, I was ready to vow on my whole seventeen years of life to destroy every last one of your kind. But what do tentacles have to do with *nikujaga*?"

"See, the thread konjac looks like tentacles, doesn't it?"

She popped the lid open. Inside was a delicious-looking meat and potato stew. Both the carrots and potatoes looked excellently seasoned—it looked exquisite.

But there was a lot more konjac in it than there should have been.

"I'm sorry, but I don't think I'll be able to eat your *nikujaga* after what you just said."

"Oh, no, no, don't mention it; please take home as much *nikujaga*—I mean tentacles—as you want, I insist."

"*Nikujaga* was the right word! Please just forget about the tentacles!"

"Come in, come in. Come eat my *nikujaga*."

Even though she had already finished with her tentacles—er, dinner, she was inviting him inside.

He forgot about the tentacle issue for a moment and timidly reached out to take a bite.

"This is so good! It tastes like it was made at home and not at a restaurant, but you need to be incredibly skilled to make something like this. Only a very old-fashioned eatery could pull this off!"

"Heh-heh-heh. Once the archbishop shows off her domestic talents, most men fall head over heels. Well, I won't be doing anything untoward today, so no need to worry!"

Anyone's heart would flutter if they heard she was as beautiful as an idol and could also cook this well. Ryouta resisted, since his first crush, Ouka, was still in his heart, but if not for her, maybe he would've gone all the way and let the archbishop drink his blood.

"Oh, and how have things been after about a week living with Shiren?" Alfoncina looked to Ryouta with a suggestive expression.

"Nothing's happened. It just tires me out. Was your whole point just to ask me that?"

"It is my duty to look after her family, after all. Come on, tell me anything."

She was telling him to get things off his chest, so Ryouta honestly revealed how tired he was.

"This is the first time in my life women haven't been weirdly friendly with me. That's why I think I got my hopes up."

"But in the end, Shiren has turned out to be too much—is that what you mean? Just tell me everything. I'll give you some nonalcoholic beer."

"She's really awful!"

In short, it wasn't the Sacred Blood Empire lifestyle that was wearing on him; it was Shiren specifically.

He had to do the full range of cleaning, cooking, and laundry that day as well, and he also went out shopping. And when it was finally time for him to rest at night, she made him go out to buy some jam bread. He just wanted a break.

With Alfoncina in front of him, all his pent-up grudges and hard feelings came pouring out. Wait, he felt kind of drunk. Was this really nonalcoholic?

"I thought so. I knew this would happen."

Alfoncina followed along, pouring something that said *daiginjo* into her own cup. It might have been some kind of sake, but he ignored it.

"Argh, now that I'm laying it all out here, Shiren really is a monster! Just help me with the chores! I did a search yesterday and learned that almost no Sacred Blooded masters shove everything off on their minions! Just this evening, she made me go out to buy jam bread for no reason!"

The more he talked, the more his frustration toward Shiren burst out of him.

"I was literally just thinking about how I could spend a long time as a minion. But I was wrong. I just want out of this country! I want to go back to Japan!"

Ugh, this kid not only can't hold his drink, but he's an angry drunk… This isn't good… As he spoke, Alfoncina remembered something. At the end of the day, she'd called him in to let off some steam, like someone would help out a new hire who was overly stressed. With as many underlings as she had, Alfoncina saw this a lot. And the sake was real sake.

But with the way this is going, I feel like he'll eventually say, That's it; I'm quitting!

She had to do something. "Hmm, I understand how you feel, Ryouta... But I think you should let her have this. See, despite the way she acts, Shiren can be a lonely person..."

"I've made up my mind! I'm not going to be her minion anymore! I'm going back to Japan!"

Internally, Alfoncina was starting to freak out. *Oh no, oh no, oh no.*

Ryouta regretted it slightly once he said it, too, but once the words had left his mouth, there was no taking it back.

That's right. There was no need to force himself. He could just escape. He'd made some friends while he was here, but he could just go see them properly once the two countries had worked out their diplomatic relations.

"But I don't recommend escape. That's suicide, you know."

She was right. He would inevitably have to go to the mountain in order to cross the border into Japan. There was a very real risk of his being attacked by another Sacred Blooded like Shiren. What could he do...?

"Look, once our field trip is over tomorrow, you'll have both Saturday and Sunday off, so why don't you relax? Take a rest; take a breather."

"What field trip?" He had been so tired out, he hadn't checked the next day's schedule.

"It said we have a field trip on the public information board. It seems we'll be going to see the border at the mountain peak."

A visit to the border? That was it. "I could get back to Japan if I jumped over the border there!"

I think...I just gave a rope to a suicidal boy...

The next day, Alfoncina was so down that even her accompanying minions started getting worried.

"Where were you wandering off to, Ryouta?! Why did it take you more than an hour to go to a store not five minutes away?! Ugh! And you reek of alcohol! You're a high schooler—what are you doing?!"

Just as he expected, Shiren was angry with him when he got home.

"The archbishop summoned me. She gave me some tentacles—I mean, *nikujaga*." He placed the containers of the stew into the fridge so they could eat it tomorrow. "And three jam breads. I'll leave them out on the kitchen so you can just eat them whenever you get hungry."

"O-okay…"

Ryouta was so candid about everything, there wasn't much more that Shiren could complain about.

"Hey, Ryouta, you can sleep in until seven tomorrow."

"I'm not gonna have enough time to make lunch if I sleep until seven."

"No, it's fine. As thanks for the jam bread, I'll make an extra-special lunch for you tomorrow. *I'm* making lunch tomorrow, okay? Don't bother me!"

"…Yeah, sure, fine."

Shiren felt a little uneasy with the way Ryouta was acting.

That night, Ryouta crept into Shiren's room as she slept. He wasn't here to feel her up; he was here to check the map of Empire territory (read: a map of Akinomiya) that hung on the wall on the other side of her bed.

Sure enough, there were a few border checkpoints within the mountain for imports and exports.

If he could sneak into the mountain around those parts, then he might be able to escape back to Japan.

There were plenty of things he didn't like about Japan as well. He had to deal with the crazy Kiyomizu, and his sister being who she was, she apparently had taken off work the entire time he was gone. Well, as long as she wasn't getting fired.

But at least he was going home to his life.

He felt so irritated when he was around Shiren—plus, she had Tamaki and Alfoncina to keep an eye on her.

She still has friends at the end of the day. She asked me not to leave her alone, but she's not alone at all. I'm the one who's alone.

This little life they had together would eventually break down anyway, so he would put an end to it now.

"Thanks, Ryouta."

But just as he was thinking about ending their relationship, he heard Shiren whisper to him.

He shrunk back. If he woke her, then he'd have to come up with a very good reason why he was in her room.

"And I'm sorr… *Zzz…zzz…*"

"Oh, you're just a sleep talker."

Phew. I didn't wake her up.

But he didn't understand why he felt so sorry hearing what she said.

"Yaaawn."

"You've been yawning way too much. I told you, you didn't have to make lunch."

They had just left school on the field trip, but Shiren had already yawned five times that day.

Each class left together for the field trip, but they weren't forced to walk in lines, so everyone bunched up with their friends.

There was no one around Ryouta and Shiren. Tamaki would glance back at Ryouta from a distance every once in a while, but that was it.

They're treating us like an official class couple… Well, that won't matter for much longer, though.

"Yaaawn. I bet this lunch is gonna knock your socks off later. *Yaaawn."*

Shiren praised herself with an odd look. For Ryouta, he was on his way back to Japan. If anything, it would be easier for him to make up his mind if Shiren just started acting the villain.

This is your fault. You're the selfish one…

But of all days, today had to be the one where she was in a good mood.

"Oh, look at that bakery. That is a very well-known shop within the Empire. The owner's nosebleed loaf incorporates blood from the nose in the dough—it's so popular, it sells out within an hour of opening. The exquisite combination of doughy sweetness and metallic saltiness makes for an addictive combination."

"I'm not going! I will never go!"

He'd decided to disregard all food and drink that had blood in it. Well, he had no intention of discriminating against the cultural regions of the world that used pig or sheep blood in their cooking, but nose blood was a hard no for him.

"That soba shop is famous, too. They succeeded in bringing out a unique umami flavor and body by putting nose blood into the broth. The farm-fresh wasabi is great, too."

"Yep, not going there, either!"

"Ooh! That ramen place there has a nose blood—"

"Is there anything you *don't* season with nose blood?!"

As they walked through town, he found there weren't any proper restaurants. "But I guess they're not going to be catering to Japanese people... *Sigh...*"

He was right—it was almost impossible for a Japanese person to live in this country. Before he knew it, Ryouta was staring at the ground.

When they left the populated area, they immediately found themselves among rice fields. The city of Akinomiya had always had a rich agricultural industry.

"Ooh, look at these fields! This view is in the *100 Places to Remember of the Empire*. Take in the beauty before you!"

"It's just a regular field. It's the Empire that's decided it's worth remembering."

Then a single frog leaped out from the stalks—

—and landed straight on Shiren's shoe.

"F-f-f-f-f-frog, frog!!! Aaaaaaaaahhhhhhhhhhhhh!!!"

Shiren reacted with a melodramatic display of terror and flailed, collapsing to the ground and rolling around. Ryouta stood by her, shocked by her absurd overreaction.

"I give up, I give up! Time out, time out! I surrender! Wh-what do you want?! Money? I'll give you as much money as you want! So get out; go away!"

Like a pinned wrestler, Shiren slapped the ground with her hand.

"I don't care how scared you are of frogs; this is ridiculous! You even started making *me* scared of them!"

"I'll give you my minion, so please leave me alone!"

"Don't hand me over to the amphibians!"

"I thought I told you. I can't stand things that are all slimy..."

"I thought you just meant things like okra or *nameko* mushrooms…"

The frog, by the way, hopped right past Shiren and back into the rice field.

"*Pant, pant…* It might come after us again, so you go first…"

"I could, but that's not really going to—"

Ryouta's hand was halfway extended when it froze in the air.

It felt strange being kind to her after deciding he was going to leave. Instead, he called out to Tamaki nearby. "Let's go." He would be managing his own long chain now.

"Oh, um, okay…I get it. That makes me glad, but I guess…I guess I will only ever be second to Fuyukura… Ha-ha-ha, of course that makes me happy, though…"

Her response made it hard for him to tell if she was happy or sad.

"But Fuyukura does seem happy to be with you after all, Ryouta. I've never seen her so lively and playful before." Tamaki smiled, impressed.

"That's lively and playful? She's always like that at home."

That was also exactly why her total lack of consideration for him had caught him so off guard.

"I see… But you seem to be having quite a bit of fun yourself, Ryouta."

"Fun? Me? Nah… I might have a collar around my neck, but I'm not a masochist."

Mentioning the collar didn't really make his argument any more convincing.

"Hold on—now that I think about it, you and Shiren don't really talk at all during school. You're not on bad terms, are you?" Ryouta asked her. Well, Shiren *had* introduced them on the first day of school, so they couldn't hate each other that much…

"No, we're on good terms. But I'm a chicken, and a weak, feeble caterpillar…"

It seemed as though Tamaki would always and forever be negative, so he would stop commenting on it.

"I guess Shiren tends to stand apart from the rest…"

Who *was* she friends with in her class anyway?

After walking for an hour afterward, they came to the border just in front of the mountain.

The Self-Defense Force was keeping watch on the land on the Japan side.

"This is the most important point within the Empire. Almost important as pineapple is to sweet-and-sour pork."

"Those can exist fine without each other!"

"Wait, you don't like sweet-and-sour pork with pineapple? Or *nikujaga* with peas?"

"I've decided I'm going to stop talking to you about food."

Sure enough, there were long rows of trucks flowing in and out of the border.

If he just took a few steps forward, he'd be back in Japan. Ryouta's hopes were slowly building.

Luckily, since he didn't get any service on his phone here, he wasn't getting creepy texts from Kiyomizu.

Yesterday, including all the texts that were basically variations on *I will be with you soon, my darling. In my birthday suit, if all goes well*, he got a total of 237 messages from her.

He wanted to mark it all as spam, but he'd have to see her in person once he went back to Japan, and that would be awkward.

"Why are there so many trucks?"

"Trade. Not only is Empire territory unfortunately not very big, it's completely landlocked by Japan. So we currently import various daily necessities from Japan."

"Wait, I thought Japan hasn't recognized this country as a sovereign nation?"

"You're right. Japan calls everyone who lives here Japanese, and the government can't legally allow their own citizens to starve. That is why they send us so much."

"But do the Japanese gain anything from this?"

"There is apparently some sort of deal with some Japanese politicians. The Emperor is a very tolerant type."

"Cool. Well, from what you just said, it sounds like the Emperor can get away with anything."

"—Hey." She tugged on his collar. "I see that nostalgia in your eyes when you look at the Japan side. Don't even joke about running over there. You are a subject of the Empire and my minion, okay?"

"I—I know."

At some point, he must have gotten laser focused on the other side.

It was obviously impossible for him to march right over the border, but it seemed relatively easy to slip into Japan through the nearby mountain.

He would have to make a clean break for it without Shiren noticing.

"All right, it looks like we're headed to our lunch spot soon. I'll show you what a traditional Sacred Blooded lunch looks like—I put my all into it. It's free if you finish within a half hour!"

"Don't deny me the chance to really taste your food. And don't take my money!"

It scared him because he knew that Shiren would actually try to do that.

"I don't need your money. It's all right so long as you feel obligated to me for the rest of eternity."

"Still a pretty steep price, if you ask me!"

Well... It would look bad on him if he didn't eat the lunch she made for him, so he decided he'd escape afterward.

Their lunch spot was a ten-minute walk away from the border, at a little plaza that faced the mountain. If he could sneak into the trees behind them, then it should be easy for him to reach Japan.

"You seem rather restless today, Ryouta."

He froze. He was showing his hand again. "It's fine; I'll just need to use the bathroom soon."

"Okay... It might be embarrassing, but if you feel anything out of the ordinary, you go straight to the urologist."

"That's really none of your business."

"We're eating now. There's a bench over there."

There were several wooden benches at the other end of the plaza. Ryouta sat down next to Shiren.

This is new, Ryouta thought.

Shiren, being herself, was humming some sort of tune.

"—Hey, that's that cover the Emperor made! Stop!"

"You blockhead. I'm just excited about eating lunch in the great outdoors."

Now that he thought about it, Ryouta had never eaten alone with a girl.

That was because if he ever chose just one to eat with, it would create trouble among the other girls later.

"Hurry up and open your lunch box. It's a fabulous traditional Sacred Blooded meal. Eat it and weep."

Shiren handed a box to Ryouta, one that was a whole size bigger than her own and meant for men. He saw a slight shadow over her face.

"Let me tell you now—if you seasoned anything with blood, I'm not eating it."

"How rude. I have made it to suit my minion's tastes."

The contents were fancier than he expected.

Fried mackerel, Japanese omelet, fried chicken, *kamaboko*, spinach boiled in soy sauce, pickled turnips, potato salad, dried purple *shiso* over rice, and pieces of pineapple and orange—all mixed together in a heap.

"Do the Sacred Blooded have some kind of saying like *Once it's in your stomach, it's all the same* or something?"

"……I was going to put them neatly in their own compartments, but I messed up the presentation, so I gave up and made it fried-rice style. Just give it a try—it will be delicious, I'm sure."

Ryouta took a bite.

"Wow…! The grassy scent of the mackerel clings to the *kamaboko*, and then you can taste the lingering sourness of the pickles along with the dry texture of the rice."

"Okay, tell me if it's good or not. I'm worried."

"It's awful." He didn't even have to think about it.

"All my hard work…," she murmured in utter defeat.

"Obviously. This is what happens when you mix it all together, even if you did make all the individual dishes properly."

"If only I had presentation skills… Next time Shenlong comes back to life, my wish will be for greater skills at presentation."

"You don't need the galaxy's most dramatic wish-giver for something so mundane!"

"Yes. I'll work even harder… A master needs to work to improve herself, too."

Something felt unusual about this whole thing to Ryouta—Shiren was oddly down today.

"But they're good on their own, right?! I put in a lot of love when I made it!"

"Er, love...?"

When Ryouta repeated the word, Shiren's face grew bright red, and her shoulders jumped in a little spasm. "It's—it's just a figure of speech! ...Ryouta? There's something I want to tell you."

"Hmm? What is it?"

He would be going soon anyway. It didn't matter what she said to him.

But when their eyes met, Shiren seemed to falter. "Uh... Yeah, I can just tell you later. Not now..."

"Then I'll hear it later."

In fact, he'd probably never hear what she wanted to say. He would be leaving this country. This was his big chance.

If someone truly subjugated him, then he would never be able to leave... Alfoncina could summon him after just a little nibble, after all.

And once that happened, he'd probably never see Ouka again.

"I'm gonna run to the bathroom real quick..." He intentionally made sure not to look at Shiren.

Once he was sure he was outside her field of vision, he finally stepped foot into the trees.

Now that he thought back, this was close to where he came out when he first left the mountain. He walked close to the border, but there were people who looked like soldiers stationed all along it. Near the plaza, however, it was completely unguarded. People there probably wouldn't be able to relax with a bunch of boorish soldiers nearby.

But then a feeling of menace sent a chill running down his spine.

What was that? He didn't think anyone was nearby, so maybe it was just his imagination.

He just kept pressing forward until he couldn't feel the danger anymore. Yeah, he had definitely imagined it.

And so he would be leaving the Sacred Blood Empire behind.

Good-bye, Shiren.

But then he heard the grass rustling before him, and something leaped out at him.

"Wha…?!" Ryouta could barely speak.

It was a small girl in a gas mask, carrying a gigantic cube-shaped rucksack on her back. She had a thick black jacket and a delicate white skirt. Maybe she was a part of some unusual squadron or something.

Neither could move, not sure of what to do after running into each other.

"I-I'm gonna die…"

After a few moments, Ryouta stepped back. He wasn't sure who she was, but he knew she wasn't someone he should've run into. She probably wasn't in the mountains picking vegetables dressed like that, that's for sure.

Luckily, he didn't sense any malice from the gas mask.

"Wait, wait, what…? No way, to think we would meet here… The power of love *is* real! Ahhh, the world really does belong to us!"

He had heard that voice somewhere before—and it was not one he wanted to hear now.

The gas mask popped off to reveal the unmistakable face of one of his Japanese classmates—Kiyomizu Jouryuuji.

Out of all the girls in the world, this one was probably the most obsessed with Ryouta. She looked like a little girl with her long black hair and straight bangs (popularly known as the princess cut), but she was actually the same age as Ryouta.

When she was with the boys in her class, the police would often ask if she was being kidnapped because of how young she looked. Ryouta had been questioned almost five times in his lifetime. She was nothing but trouble, so he wanted her to stay away.

"Just as I mentioned in my text this morning, I've finally come all the way to this foreign land to find you. But I never thought we'd meet so quickly. This just confirms that our love is infinite."

"Wait, you weren't just making stuff up…?"

It was hard for him to determine what exactly he should believe because there had been so many messages.

Being close to her was dangerous, so he slowly backed away.

"Oh, there's something I want to show you. It's a new game about you. It went on sale two days ago."

Kiyomizu held out a PS-style case that said *Ryou-Plus* on it.

"I solicited a big-name game developer to make it, and it's finally finished. Now with this, I can boldly walk through town and whisper *You're so cute* and *I love you* to you. I've only just passed thirty hours of play so far, but you and I are already head over heels in love with each other. We'll be going to Atami next. And the eighteen-plus, only-for-adults version called *Ryou-Plus: Ecstasy* will finally be going on sale next month!"

"Okay, there's a lot I need to say, so I'll just take this one piece at a time. First, I don't remember ever giving you permission to make a game like that, not even in a past life. And this isn't an indie game, but a nationwide release, right? What's the point of broadcasting me to the whole damn country? Oh, and I hate to pick at the small details, but how long are you playing in a single day?"

"I make sure to play in a brightly lit area so my eyes don't get tired, and I only play fifteen hours a day."

"You're completely nuts!"

"Oh, and I'm already thinking about merchandising. Work on the anime adaptation began during the game development. Airing of all twenty-four episodes will start on the fourth next month at one thirty AM on cable. I also want to record some extras for the DVD release, so I would appreciate your help in that."

An odd pain seized Ryouta, and he felt like crying.

Ryouta's power typically only ever had an effect on girls he met in person. Despite his grandfather's "curse," it didn't have the power to make women fall in love with him just by seeing his name. As long as he could keep away from the women around him, he could still somehow manage.

But ever since meeting Kiyomizu, things were different.

The temple that Kiyomizu's family owned was super-rich due to some commercial law for prayer or whatever, and they used their financial power to make Ryouta Asagiri merchandise to sell in school. The number of girls targeting him exploded because of that, making it more and more dangerous for him to walk around town on the weekends.

"I guess the danger to my virtue is at the national level now…"

He was at his wit's end. Once he got back to Japan, he would have to start thinking about emigrating to another country.

"Whatever, I'm out of tears. I want to go back to Japan, so could you tell me if you know the way?"

"No, we must spend more precious alone time before you go back."

She produced some sort of pipe and blew into it toward Ryouta.

"Ow!"

There was a sting on his arm—a needle had pierced his skin. His strength immediately drained away, leaving him completely immobile.

"What is…this…?"

"A self-defense weapon," she said lightly.

"Why are you walking around with that…? And why did you prick me…?"

"Don't you know already?"

Kiyomizu dropped her bag and removed her jacket. There was some kind of small, round paper lantern on her blouse underneath, like something a monk practicing asceticism in the mountains would wear. As she slowly removed the outfit, she revealed a black bra covering her practically flat chest… There was something weird about this!

"I'm here for your body, Ryouta… Eh-heh."

She was taking off her own clothes, but her face was red for some reason.

Now he remembered! Kiyomizu was the one who was always after him physically!

"Calm down, Kiyomizu! There's crazy bugs and poisonous trees in the mountains. You should cover as much of your skin as possible! And that bra looks *really* bad on you! You're fine with just a sports bra!"

"Heh-heh-heh, I've decided to give up on trying to convince you with orthodox methods, and I knew very well that you would be trying to sneak through. No one will interrupt us here—it's perfect. We can enjoy our amorous adventure here, alone. It will be just like a Harlequin manga. Not that I've ever read any."

She then removed her skirt, then her socks. She was completely in her underwear.

"I am a woman who will do what I say. I will take you as my own in my

©Hiroki Ozaki

birthday suit. Oh, I should take a picture of you every minute along the way. *Click!*"

A half-naked Kiyomizu approached Ryouta and started removing his clothes.

He wanted to fight back, but the poison seemed to have a powerful, immediate effect, so he could barely do anything. It was as if he were physically bound.

Alfoncina had given him poison the other day as well—this was becoming a pattern.

"I-I'm going to be raped... And this all looks like I'm the offender here..."

"No, we are both consenting here. We just have a little difference in opinion."

"If our opinions are different, it's not consent!"

"Give me the right to do naughty things to you, and then I'll stop."

It was a childish stretch of an argument.

"This is the first thing that's happening to me when I try to leave the Empire? Is this my punishment...?"

Ryouta sighed.

It was his punishment for abandoning Shiren.

He wondered what it was that she had wanted to say.

"First, we'll start with a kiss... This is actually my first kiss. Ryouta, please take my first." Kiyomizu slowly reached out to Ryouta's cheeks. She seemed a little awkward for having come this far—maybe she was shy. If it was at all possible, he wanted her to be too shy to move on to anything else.

"Hmm...? What's this wound on your arm? It's like you've been bitten by something..."

He had an even worse feeling than he'd had before.

That wound was from Alfoncina XIII.

"Oh, there's also a bite mark on your neck...several of them."

Those were from Shiren. She would bite him every night the moment he let his guard down, so his neck was in bad shape.

"Could this be a bite from when they were whispering sweet nothings to each other in their chambers...? He's bitten in so many places; this can't be a coincidence… And this collar… And so the conclusion I come to is that Ryouta's purity has been sullied by the vampires……………………………"

The shock seemed too much for her to handle, and Kiyomizu froze. She sat like a statue, still clinging to Ryouta.

"Hey, Kiyomizu, are you okay? Are you dead? I mean, I'm not going to ask you to die, maybe just lose all your memories from the shock."

"…My apologies. I was only lost in thought a little. I was thinking about what I should do if God were desecrated by the vampires. I believe this means my job is to remove as much of the taint as I can. That is all I can do."

Her hand was already on his boxers.

"Wait. I'm not pure or dirty or anything! I just got bitten!"

"I don't need your lies. Um…am I really not that cute to you?" Kiyomizu looked at Ryouta with worry.

"I—I mean, I guess you are…"

He couldn't lie about that.

Kiyomizu was definitely a girl with issues, but that didn't make her not cute. She was good-looking enough for some guys with issues to create a group called "Protectors of Kiyomizu and Her Small Tits."

"I'm glad… Then don't a beautiful girl and a beautiful boy make a nice couple together?"

A smile bloomed across Kiyomizu's face. He hated to say it, but it was a cute expression.

"Then become one with me. I will be taking this off, too."

There was nothing he could do, since he couldn't move. There was nowhere for him to run…

But then came the sound of feet rustling through the grass. Someone was running toward them.

And just as his boxers were about to slip off—

"Don't go touching other people's minions! Don't expect me to go easy on you!"

—Shiren leaped toward them.

"Shiren…"

"Ryouta, are you okay? You were taking really long in the bathroom, so I came after you. I remembered what happened with the archbishop, so I got scared and came to check on you! I won't make the same mistake twice!"

Ryouta had been saved by Shiren's wit.

"And for some reason, I had a feeling you were going to go pretty far away."

Her words stung him in the chest. That was exactly what he was trying to do.

"But to think you'd be attacked by some woman again. Come on, Ryouta, we're going back." She took his arm.

"Please wait. Who are *you*?! Ryouta will be going home to Japan!" Kiyomizu pulled on him from the opposite direction.

"Hey, let go, little elementary kid." Shiren pulled on him harder.

"I refuse. *You* let go, middle schooler! And I am a high school student, thank you!" Kiyomizu pulled back against her. And of course, Ryouta's arms stretched in both directions. It hurt.

"What?! You can't be a high schooler, looking like that! You can't skip grades in Japan! And I am in high school, too! I will bite you the next time you call me a middle schooler!"

"Stop! You're gonna rip me in half! I can't stretch anymore! Seriously, I'm gonna break!"

"Ryouta is hurt, so let go. I own him."

"I am just carrying out the simple job of returning a Japanese citizen to his home country. You should let go!"

"No! I don't want to be alone anymore!" Shiren's cry rang out through the trees. "I've been all alone since this country was created! I don't want to be treated that way anymore! I want friends, too! I want someone who'll talk to me!"

He remembered Shiren calling Tamaki Shijou her only comrade.

Shiren had never called anybody her friend.

Had anybody ever interrupted them when he'd been talking to her? Even that very day on their field trip, had Shiren talked to anybody besides Ryouta?

Shiren didn't want a reverent domestic helper. What she needed was an equal, someone she could relax with and blow off steam.

It had taken this long for Ryouta to notice.

"By the way, Ryouta, who is this girl?"

"I've come a long distance to obliterate the parasites known as the Sacred Blooded."

Both of them dropped Ryouta when Kiyomizu spoke, and their standoff started again.

Kiyomizu's eyes grew sharp, and she then put her hand in her bra. A moment later, she pulled out a set of rings on several of her fingers, metal spikes protruding from them. She had a hidden weapon.

"I'm sorry—I have no intention of going easy on a Sacred Blooded. I will annihilate you with my own power."

"I see; you're a member of the Virginal Father."

"The Virginal Father? That was the assassin's group mentioned in our textbook... I didn't think they were real... Wait, you're one of them, Kiyomizu?!"

"Yes, we are a global organization that aims to protect the purity of humanity. We've mixed ourselves in with religious communities all over the world to lend a hand in exterminating these parasites."

Slipping on protective fingerstalls, Kiyomizu smiled. Ryouta spotted a katana poking out of the box behind her when he looked more closely at it. She was armed to the teeth.

"So you came here to wipe out the Sacred Blood Empire..."

"No, I came to see you, Ryouta darling. I'll only deal with the Sacred Blooded along the way."

"Does your organization know or care how sloppy you are about this?!"

Feeling a little ignored, Shiren interjected. "You certainly are bold to underestimate the Sacred Blooded. I, Shiren Fuyukura, will quickly show you what our people can do! You cannot hold a candle to us!"

"Fuyukura?" Kiyomizu reacted to her last name.

"Yes. I will be making Ryouta my minion in the future. He's not officially mine yet, though..."

"I'm impressed, Ryouta. She might be a parasite, but she has such high standing."

"High standing? What's so high standing about Shiren?"

"Now, come at me. I can deal with you with my bare hands." Shiren stepped forward, unarmed.

"Stop! You don't have to fight!" Ryouta yelled, still paralyzed.

Kiyomizu had the build of a little girl, but she was armed with dangerous weapons. This would probably end up as more than just a petty quarrel.

"Heh-heh-heh. There is no way for you to win. My training *yuigesa* overcoat and skirt are specially made to burn the skin of the Sacred Blooded if they touch it. It is a concentration of the essences that make up the prayer and magic of my denomination—this ordinary fabric is filled with the automation of farming and fishing of the head temple of a just, heretical, genuine, fierce love and courage of overwhelming, strongest, unrivaled, Olympian, new-age miracles of Buddha with Academy Award–level power! In short, you are at a great disadvantage in this fight, Sacred Blooded!"

"Erm... You sort of lost me with all the adjectives, but you're essentially saying I'll be in trouble if I touch your clothes, right?"

"Indeed! I shall kill you!"

"But you're not wearing any clothes."

The temperature in the air plummeted for a moment.

Kiyomizu was wearing only a bra and panties. Her clothes were behind her, tossed aside.

"Ryouta, did you know this was going to happen, so you took my clothes...?"

"Your strike zone is way too low, Ryouta..."

"You took your own clothes off! Stop making stuff up! And you're way off base here, Shiren!"

"It is not to my advantage to fight in my underwear. If my bra were to rip during battle, things might end up a little steamy. I don't mind Ryouta seeing, but I will not stand for this parasite looking at me."

That was a stupid thing to worry about.

"I will return to Japan for today. But I will be back, so long as I hold love for you, darling Ryouta. So long as *S——e-san* keeps airing. Then I will take you back."

"Quit pretending we're in love! Quit it!"

"We will battle together one day, Shiren Fuyukura. I will extinguish the Imperial blood with my own hands."

Kiyomizu hauled the large rucksack onto her back, then disappeared into the mountains like a ninja.

In her underwear.

Apparently, she'd forgotten about her clothes. Well, whatever.

"I'll make an exception for you and let you go, since you know Ryouta. Don't ever show yourself to us again."

Shiren put her hands on her hips with a smug look.

Well, at least she was acting normal. Ryouta felt a bit relieved. *She just likes acting important—*

But then Shiren's neutral expression crumpled, as if it had just been painted on.

Now she looked like a girl who'd had more than enough of the fear of being alone.

"Don't go anywhere anymore, Ryouta!"

She embraced him. No—clung to him. Desperately, as if she would never let go. "Didn't you make a promise at the beginning? That you would never leave me alone?! Keep your promises! Keep them! I won't stand for it if you don't!"

"You don't have any friends, do you, Shiren?"

He took her silence as a yes.

"There was something I couldn't tell you earlier, Ryouta."

"Oh yeah, there was."

"I'm sorry."

Shiren's head drooped, her voice dejected. She seemed genuinely sorry, from the bottom of her heart.

"I'm sorry for making you go out and buy bread yesterday. I was just being selfish. When you were late getting home, I realized what I'd done. I was worried something had happened to you. Really worried… But I couldn't go out and search for you…"

That was why she felt as though she had to go out and find him straightaway—she worried she would lose him; she explained as much with a hoarse voice.

"Stay by my side. You don't have to cook or clean if you don't want to. Just stay with me. Talk to me about stupid stuff, be annoyed when I talk too much, make fun of me. That's an order. Follow it to the letter."

Shiren had been all alone. In a way, she was like him.

If he went back to Japan now, he wouldn't be able to sleep at night.

"Yeah, I know."

"Thank you, Ryouta."

"So…can you let go of me now? Uh…I'm still not really dressed."

Shiren realized and immediately leaped back from Ryouta.

Things could take a turn for the worse if she kept hugging him while he was half-naked. Ryouta himself might end up taking it the wrong way, too.

"This is just, um, a trick of your mind…"

"I know. By the way, Kiyomizu said something about Imperial blood—what did she mean?"

After Shiren spent a moment in silence with a guilty look—

"My full name is Shiren Elisabeta Alexandra Florentina Sylvia Rosanna Fuyukura."

"I'd like to see you try writing *that* on a form. Oh, wait, I know that name…"

He remembered it was unique to the women in the Imperial family. It was in the history textbook.

"Yeah, I'm the previous emperor's daughter, and my big sis…my *venerable* elder sister is the current emperor," Shiren said breezily.

"Wait a sec… That means if something happened to the Emperor, you'd be next in line for the throne… I don't think I'm even allowed to speak casually to you…"

Ryouta was paralyzed after hearing who Shiren really was. Of course she'd be acquainted with the archbishop.

"That solves the mystery of why you're so over-the-top arrogant. But still, why do you live in a house like that?"

It was just a little house; the Imperial Fuyukura family wouldn't live there, would they?

"My mother is pure Japanese, so that means half of my blood is the same as yours, Ryouta. After a whole bunch of people tried to assassinate my father, my mother ran away and went missing. Some say they were both killed, but the more convincing argument was that my mother was a Japanese spy who ran away after killing him," Shiren calmly explained, her eyes cold and emotionless.

Her explanation of the tragedy was clear and thorough—meaning she was used to talking about it.

"That is why I would never fit in at the Sacred Blood Imperial Palace, and that's why I took my mother's last name of Fuyukura as a commoner…"

Dispirited, Shiren added:

"And that's why I was alone. I'm the daughter of a criminal. I guess that makes me a criminal, too."

But for her crime, there was no atonement.

Sacred Blooded
First Cathedral Year Calendar

January 1-3	Holiday
February 3	Setsubun (Bean-Throwing Festival)
Golden Week	Holiday
June 6	New Swimsuit Line Showcase
July 7	Tanabata (Star Festival)
December 25	Christmas Celebration

Here's the gist of it.

Wait, what's that in June?

And we don't do anything on the New Year because we're taking it off.

Yes! It's so important not to do anything sometimes. Humans need their holidays!

You are ALWAYS on holiday!

EPISODE 4
LET'S MEET THE SACRED BLOODED EMPEROR!

"What on Earth could you possibly need on a Saturday, Ryouta? I didn't think you'd call me out so suddenly. And it's just me...alone? Have I said something unnecessary, and that's why you invited me...? Is this a blood punishment...? I'm sorry; please don't hit me—my father now isn't the type of person to do that! ...But if you're not going to, then...then maybe the reason you called me out on a weekend was to tell me that you... Kya!"

Tamaki, at their meeting place in the school, seemed restless.

Ryouta had come by himself from the Fuyukura household to the library.

Shiren must have felt somewhat uncomfortable announcing that she was the Emperor's little sister the day before, so when Ryouta said he was going to the library to study on his own, she gave him a quick okay. She probably wanted to be alone, too.

He felt a little scared walking around without the chain on the collar, but the collar was apparently enough to show tentative ownership. If someone did force him down and drink his blood, it'd be all over, though.

"Sorry, I just had to see you, Shijou."

"Oh my gosh, are you really going to confess to me...? Were you proposing to me, back there in the store...?"

"Like I said in my text, I want to get into the library to do some research."

"Oh, um...that's right. I apologize, as an eternal waste of human space, for having such expectations... *Sigh*, I can't wait for the sweet embrace of death..."

Tamaki had gotten herself excited, and now she was getting herself down.

"I have a key, so I can take you anywhere you need to go. Actually, you will get lost if I don't take you. People who go in without a member of the library committee never return."

"What kind of dungeon is this?!"

But when they went in, he found that Tamaki wasn't lying at all.

There were several rows of bookshelves, but there were also stacked piles of books walling off some of the spaces between the shelves. The aisles were impassable, literally buried in books.

"This library is on the high school campus, but it also acts as the national library. We are currently undertaking a mass rearrangement of our collection to obtain any material related to the Sacred Blooded, so that's why everything looks like this. To be honest, it's not very good for my mental health because the books always look like they're going to fall over. Well, no one would mourn if my life were scattered to the winds, though."

"I hate to interrupt your tragic soliloquy, but can I ask you about a book?"

"Sure. As long as you're okay asking an unloved garbage heap like me, then please ask me anything."

She wasn't just being a pessimist; she also seemed to be pouting.

"Where could I find a book on the assassination of the previous emperor?"

Tamaki looked surprised, but she knew exactly what he was really after. "I understand now. You want to do research on Fuyukura, don't you?"

"Right. She told me you understood her. I want you to help me."

The Sacred Blooded history section was in a corner with an unstable tower of books.

"A great deal of books detailing the deeds of the previous emperor were published around the time the Empire was created. This is a small country, so by *published*, I also count self-published things like fanzines that only printed fifty or a hundred copies. That's why the quality is mixed, from the very best to the very worst. The Sacred Blooded can be very attached to their self-published works."

"Okay, as long as I get the circumstances, then."

The assassination of the previous emperor was an important event, so even after reading just a few volumes, he got the gist of it. He thought he remembered reading about it online as well, but it was such a gruesome incident, he subconsciously forgot about it.

"The previous emperor fell in love with a Japanese woman who wasn't his wife, and Shiren was their child, huh? His name isn't written anywhere here, though."

"His Majesty's last name is so venerable, it cannot be published. His first name is the same, and we can only write the names of emperors starting three rulers ago. The previous emperor's lover was Sairi Fuyukura. Hers is the most detested name in this country. They say she was a member of the Virginal Father and she assassinated her lover, then went into hiding. At the very least, that is the conclusion the present highest-ranking Imperial officers have come to."

"Why would a member of the Virginal Father get romantically involved with the emperor of the Sacred Blooded?"

"It happens all the time in movies, doesn't it? Forbidden love between spy and target, and it almost always ends in tragedy... But right now, I do sort of understand how Sairi felt." Tamaki gave a passionate sigh and cast a sidelong glance at Ryouta.

"Why?"

"Well, you know, that's, um... Ooh...I hate how weak my heart is..."

Tamaki would slip into negative mode if he left her to her own devices, so he steered the subject back on topic.

"I guess that's why Shiren was stripped of the Imperial name, took the name Fuyukura, and began living as an ordinary person... Wait, what's so ordinary about all this?!"

Ryouta slammed another tower of books in front of him in a fit of anger.

"She's being treated like a criminal! Maybe she's not technically being discriminated against, but if they force her to live with the name Fuyukura, they're just broadcasting to everyone that she's the daughter of a woman who committed regicide! And they're just giving her a pension and telling her to make do by herself? That's awful! Of course no one will be her friend!"

It would be stranger if Shiren Fuyukura *wasn't* lonely after all that.

That was why all her classmates thoroughly avoided dealing with her.

This was different from bullying, but bullying was terrible, too. Either way, it was much too risky for any ordinary person to be associated with Shiren.

She may have been disowned by the Emperor, but she still inherited the previous emperor's blood. Getting close to her might attract the Emperor's attention, but if they attacked her, then what would happen to them if Shiren ever held power?

That was why no one even dared associate with her, and instead everyone left Shiren all alone.

They should know better. They should know that the child of a killer wasn't a killer herself.

Everyone thought of the criminal's daughter as a criminal, so much so that the daughter herself believed them, too.

"This is awful…"

He found himself whacking the book against the floor, even though a committee member was right nearby.

"I'm sorry. I was working to help her, but I ran away as well. I was afraid of the rumors I heard of people wanting to take Fuyukura's life, so I put distance between us. I really am terrible. I'm like the soldier who gets killed off at the beginning of a story to demonstrate how strong the enemy is…"

"No, it's not your fault. I mean, I get it. If someone asked you to be her friend, but actually being her friend could get you killed, of course you wouldn't be able to get close to her."

And Shiren was aware of that, too.

She knew that any person close to her would be ostracized or attacked, so she couldn't even attempt to make friends. She wasn't shy or anything. She was just very aware of the whole situation.

If there was anyone who could put a stop to this…

…it was the Emperor.

"Wouldn't this all be solved if the Emperor said her little sister was blameless?"

"Well, the Emperor is concerned about her. That's why she comes to inspect the school once every other month or so. But the hard-liners have very strong opinions, so at the moment, she is unable to do anything."

"Oh, right, the archbishop did mention something about an inspection…"

In that case, there was only one thing for him to do.

"Then the next time the Emperor comes, I'm going to ask her face-to-face. A direct appeal, if you will."

Tamaki went deathly pale.

"That's dangerous! That's suicide! In the Edo period, any peasant who lodged a complaint to their lord would one hundred percent be killed. You'll be crucified. It'll be treated as a more serious crime than any regular Sacred Blooded could commit..."

"Eh, it'll be fine. The Emperor's Shiren's big sister, right?"

He had absolutely no authority here, but he wanted to do at least this much for her.

If not, then he knew he wouldn't be able to return to Japan. He still wanted to go back, even now, but if that meant leaving Shiren behind in solitude, then that was another story.

He had been alone in Japan, so he knew her pain better than anyone else.

And so, he wanted to fulfill his duty as minion before leaving.

"No! You cannot do something so dangerous!"

Tamaki's voice echoed through the closed library, filled with an almost threatening aura he would never have imagined from someone so passive.

"It is much too risky. When has anyone ever said *It'll be fine* and then it actually was? You might be killed, your body tragically hanged on the gallows, picked at by the crows, and never able to rest in peace, your soul left to wander an endless hell. And even if you had a grave made for you, it would be knocked over immediately, and people might spit on it! Oh, how pitiful you are, Ryouta!"

"Er, I don't really need the pessimism... It makes me nervous..."

"I will do it in your stead! I will scatter my guts over the gallows!"

"I appreciate the sentiment, but you really don't have to go that far!"

"No, it is the least I can do. I believe Fuyukura has accepted me, at least a little. And...you will never, ever make a decision that might end in your death. If it ever comes to that, I will take your place!"

"Shijou, you treat me really well, but I can't put a whole life-and-death situation in your hands."

"No. I will do it. Because I...ah—"

Tamaki faltered, shrinking back slightly.

Her shoulder collided with an unstable tower of books.

"Hey, watch out!"

The books fell in an avalanche coming straight for her. And a lot of them were thick as dictionaries—this was bad!

"Ah! All the sins of my past life are finally coming for me!"

"Shijou!"

He didn't have time to hesitate. Ryouta leaped toward Tamaki. Had he never come to the library, she would never have gotten wrapped up in this. He was responsible!

"Owww... Are you okay, Shijou?" he asked, and he felt something oddly warm enveloping his body.

"Yes, I am all right..."

In their current position, it looked as if Ryouta had pushed her over.

"Sorry! I'll get out of your way!"

He didn't mention it, but her chest was pressed right against him. Her clothes made her seem more slender than she actually was, but that didn't really matter at the moment.

"You don't have to... You see... Um...I don't want your blood or anything... You are purely...important to me, so...I don't want you to risk your life..."

What was she talking about? This was getting weird.

Actually, girls had knocked him over plenty of times when he was in Japan, but this was the first time he'd done the knocking over.

Tamaki's glossy black hair rested on Ryouta's shoulder.

"Anyway, please don't put yourself in danger. Someone like you never has fortune on his side, so you will die. But if you still insist on going, then...may we do a deed as man and woman...a bloody version of a scene you'd see before the climax of a Hollywood movie?"

"W-w-w-wait, wait, I..."

"I am sorry; I will become as a wolf for five minutes. I would appreciate it if you forgot about this in an hour."

Tamaki's face was right next to Ryouta's arm.

"Now, if you don't mind me taking your left arm. Don't mind me— *Nom*."

He felt a slight pain in his left arm, and at the same time, he felt paralysis overcoming him again.

But it was different from when the archbishop bit him. That time, it had all seemed like a dream because the sensation was so sudden, but he was conscious this time. It felt as if he was losing the area that had been bitten…

"Rgh… What on Earth? It feels like my motivation is being sapped away…"

"I don't know the details, but being bitten by the Sacred Blooded produces a similar effect to that of dangerous drugs. Perhaps mine is of a depressive type? *Nom, nom…*"

A slight prickling pain ran up and down his left arm, probably because she couldn't bite the whole thing at once. It was as if she were slowly consuming his body. But it wasn't as unpleasant as he expected it to be.

Instead, it almost felt like nothing mattered anymore. Ryouta felt incredibly small, and he was beginning to want to give anything and everything to Tamaki.

"Shijou…I'm so useless, but if you're okay with that…"

"You're not useless at all. Your blood is so delicious; it's unlike anything I've ever tasted. I barely have any hopes or dreams, and I've just lived as a good student without any direction, but I finally have dreams now. Um…I will give you everything I have, so please take it."

He'd never seen such diligence and determination in Tamaki's face before. It was way different from Alfoncina, who had just enjoyed biting him indiscriminately.

"Ohhh…Ryouta, your blood is amazing."

"O-oh, thanks…"

"I am so sorry, Ryouta, but this will make you my minion…"

That was certainly how it would go according to the rules. But Alfoncina had already bitten him. How would this turn out?

He'd never been kissed, but if he counted all of Shiren's bites as one, this would be the third time he'd been bitten by a girl… This had to be some kind of new record.

"I can still keep this up for another two minutes... But it would be bad if Shiren saw us..."

That was when they heard a set of familiar footsteps.

"Ryouta, I thought it was odd you were studying so hard at the library during the day off, but now I see it was a rendezvous..."

When he looked up, Shiren was right there.

His weariness vanished in an instant. "Ahhhhhhhhhh! Noooooooooo! Shiren, I have a really, really good reason for—"

"Be more of a minion!"

The moment he rushed to his feet, he was practically countered with a punch. He flew a good distance back.

And he was once again buried under a collapsing book tower.

"Does that hurt? Know that my fist is in more pain!"

"No, I am definitely in more pain... I thought I could do something for y— Nah, never mind."

Trying to buy favors from her was a bad look. Ryouta shut his mouth.

"Oh. Ohhhhh...Fuyukura, Ryouta is not at fault here... This is all my fault... If you are going to punch anyone, please let it be me... You only need to punish me!" Tamaki pressed toward Shiren in tears.

"I can't believe you're blaming Tamaki, Ryouta. You're the worst..."

"What? It sorta sounds like I'm turning into the bad guy here..."

Words are powerful.

"How much did you bite him anyway, Tamaki?"

"Roughly between sixty and sixty-two seconds."

That was rather precise. Was it also the standard amount of time for creating a minion...?

"Okay, then he shouldn't totally be your minion, so that's not a problem. I'll hear the rest of the story from Ryouta later. I'll even allow the use of instruments of torture."

"*Allow?* You'd be the one using them!"

He wouldn't allow this at all. Ryouta decided to quickly change the subject.

"So why are you here, Shiren?"

"Are you blind, Ryouta?" Shiren quickly glanced to the side.

Standing there was a tall, stern-looking woman who didn't seem to belong at a school.

She wore armor that made her look like a knight from medieval Europe, and strapped to her back, she had an enormous sword that was practically the same size as her. Her silver hair was pulled into a ponytail so as not to get in the way.

"Um, is she a cosplayer?"

After all, the archbishop looked like a character in some anime.

"This high school seems rather lively, doesn't it?"

The lady knight placed her hand to her mouth and chuckled delicately. Her mannerisms made it clear she belonged to high society. Character-wise, she was probably better off switching with the archbishop.

"This is Lady Sasara Tatsunami, one of the Imperial guards. I'm showing her around the school."

When Shiren introduced her, Sasara Tatsunami bowed reverently. "It is a pleasure. As she said, my name is Sasara Tatsunami, a member of the Imperial Guard. As the Emperor's minion, I have come to conduct a preliminary inspection."

"Wait, you're a minion. Does that mean you're not Sacred Blooded, but human...?"

He felt a little happy, as if he'd met a fellow Japanese person overseas.

"No, I am not. I am Sacred Blooded. A Sacred Blooded bitten by her own kind can still become a minion, can she not?"

Sure, the effect of a Sacred Blooded sucking blood should still work on those of the same kind.

"On Monday, the day after tomorrow, Her Imperial Majesty will come to inspect the school, so I am here for a preliminary inspection for the occasion. We cannot have any places where an assassin might hide, can we?"

The Emperor's inspection. Ryouta tensed slightly—that would be his only chance to make his appeal.

"Of course, this room is full of unstable books, so it is not suitable for inspection." Sasara's elegant expression quickly transformed into one more imposing as she looked around.

"The knights of the Imperial Guard report directly to the Emperor, and all of them are nobility. They all need loyalty, a willingness to give up their lives for the Emperor, outstanding swordsmanship, and refinement worthy of a guard. That means the Imperial Guard are a selected elite! Oh-ho!"

"Shiren, you tend to act all big when it comes to other people's accomplishments. It's annoying, so cut it out."

She had even put her hands on her hips to show off how important she was.

"I am simply fighting for the Emperor's love. That is all. There is absolutely nothing to be proud of," said Sasara. She looked exactly how he imagined a top-tier warrior to look. It was perfect.

But he saw something that caught his attention.

"By the way, what is that you have on your belt?"

A rather large stuffed doll hung over her hip. Honestly, he thought it might get in the way of her sword. It had long hair, so it was probably of some kind of girl character.

"This is a stuffed doll of the Emperor," she answered. Kinda strange. "The Imperial Guard can never forget that no matter where or when, we are always with the Emperor. This doll is my lifeline, so that I will never forget that feeling."

"Incredible, Lady Knight! An exemplary spirit! I hope Ryouta will serve me with the same enthusiasm one day!"

Ryouta wanted to say, *Come on, think logically for a second. This girl's a little nuts*, but he decided to keep quiet. Maybe Sasara was just a single-minded person.

"I was originally thinking about getting a regular doll, but the face was not soft enough for me, so I decided to get a stuffed one."

"Yeah, I'm not sure how the Emperor would feel about that," he couldn't help but comment. He was getting the feeling that everyone in this country was a weirdo.

"Wha...? Are you trying to deny my love for our emperor...? Could you be a demon sent to test my love for her?"

The guard was reeling from his comment.

"Well, no one's said I can't say what I think..."

"Additionally, there are a total of fifteen in the Imperial Guard including

myself, and I surveyed the other fourteen. I received various opinions: 'Gross,' 'This freaks me out,' 'You crossed the line, and it's not funny anymore,' 'The Emperor's freaked out, too,' 'This is too weird,' 'I almost don't want to be friends anymore,' 'Do what you want, I guess,' 'Are you serious? You know you can't just do whatever you want, right?' 'Just quit,' 'You're an embarrassment to our country,' 'You're an insult to the rest of our species,' 'Obviously bad,' 'If you made it to adulthood, then there must be a problem with our current education system,' and 'You're dumb.'"

"All fourteen of them gave negative opinions!"

"I'm hungry. Get me a snack in five seconds!"

A woman's voice suddenly came from somewhere.

"Oh, I didn't realize I was gripping Her Imperial Majesty. Her voice box went off."

"You gave her a voice box?!"

"I'm hungry. Get me a snack in five seconds!"

"You don't have to keep playing it!"

"Well, that is all for me now. Thank you for showing me around, Fuyukura." Sasara bowed courteously, then left.

"Wasn't she incredible, Ryouta?"

"Incredibly weird, if that's what you mean," he said as Shiren hooked the chain onto his collar.

"You're finished here now, aren't you? We're going home. Don't leave your master alone."

"Oh, yeah."

Don't leave your master alone.

Those words echoed like a physical weight in his chest. He needed to work hard so that she wouldn't be alone, even without him.

But there was something Ryouta noticed about the guard that left him a little uneasy.

She called Shiren "Fuyukura"...

To the guard, Shiren was just a civilian with the last name Fuyukura.

"I will look the other way this time, Tamaki, but you will be thankful until your death that I decided to let it go."

"Isn't that kinda patronizing?!"

"I'm sorry...," Tamaki murmured. "I will cut out my tongue and die..."
That was the most negative he'd seen Tamaki so far.

"Oh, and, Ryouta," Shiren said, turning to him, "I will be hearing what
you have to say so I can torture you."

"Your method and goal are backward!"

If she was being open about having torture as the goal, he was terrified.

What would she poke and bend this time...?

"We're going now, Ryouta. Hop to it!"

She tugged sharply on his chain, and he almost fell forward headfirst.

He could tell just at a glance that she was pissed; her pigtails were practically standing straight up.

"You anger me any more, and I will drink enough of your blood to make
you anemic!"

"Stop... I'll actually pass out..."

"You are probably the sole Japanese person in the Empire, Ryouta. That's
why these mistakes happen. I understand why it happened, but...I'm still
furious."

Shiren was stewing in anger the whole way home. Ryouta was tense the
entire time, too, since he didn't know when she might suddenly bite him.

"So what were you doing with Tamaki in the library?"

The moment they got home, she got straight to the point and asked him.
She was being sincere, he could tell.

And it was hard for him to answer straight...

"Tamaki has more going for her than I do, doesn't she? Am I too childish
for you?"

For a moment, he didn't understand what she'd said.

"Huh?" Ryouta stared at her blankly, but Shiren's face was starting to
flush red.

"I—I mean, wasn't there a whole mood going on between you? We've
never had anything like that before! But I can't get into a relationship like
that with my minion..."

She was half an inch from her wit's end. A smile almost unconsciously
crossed his face.

He was starting to feel stupid for going out of his way to hide the truth.

"Shijou and I were researching the Emperor."

"...That was unnecessary." Shiren's voice suddenly dropped to almost a whisper. Her expression was unreadable—maybe she was happy, maybe she was sad, but he couldn't tell. "Ryouta, you are a hard worker, truly. You have no brain-to-mouth filter, but you are a man of action."

"Thanks."

"So you don't need to go out on the weekends."

Her voice was so quiet, he had to concentrate to catch her words.

Ryouta was slightly miffed. "What do you mean by that? Are you planning on treating me like a child? Or a slave?"

"That's not what I mean! I don't treat minions like slaves!"

"Then why are you forbidding me from going outside?"

"Because you'll go back to Japan."

Ryouta had no response for her when she said that. When she found him yesterday in the mountains, Kiyomizu had been trying to help him get away. That meant Shiren at least knew he was trying to run.

Shiren's face was devoid of color, as if she had just lost something. "You might not understand, but I don't mind my circumstances. Somebody has to bear my mother's crimes. I can survive. So if you don't mind it, I want you to stay here. I'll do the shopping. If there's something you want, I'll get it for you. So, so...don't go off on your own and leave me behind."

Before she realized it, her voice was quavering with tears.

"You'd probably want to be the minion of some other Sacred Blooded, not someone everyone hates. I get it. But I only have you. I really, truly only have you. I know this is selfish, but you have to stay... This isn't an order. Just a request."

That was how Shiren really felt, something she hadn't been able to honestly express this whole week.

She hadn't noticed how tense her fists were. He couldn't read her face from this angle, but he wasn't going to try.

"...Ryouta, is there someone you love back in Japan?"

"Yeah...there is."

It was a girl named Ouka Sarano, his first love.

"If you had the chance to go back, would you?"

Ryouta couldn't even open his mouth.

"I'm sorry." Shiren's head lowered. "Yes, I suppose you are popular. I'm just causing problems for you by not letting you go back, aren't I? I'm sorry."

Shiren was much too kind. She couldn't be selfish when it came to the most important things, and she couldn't ignore how other people felt.

She would enjoy life much more if she just didn't think about Ryouta's circumstances.

Ryouta was staring straight at her—or maybe it would be more accurate to say he couldn't look away.

But staring at her wouldn't save her.

"I'll stay at home the rest of today and tomorrow. I promise."

He'd spend those two days at home working out a draft for his appeal.

All so that Shiren wouldn't be left alone.

And then, it was Monday. Inspection day.

"I will be meeting the Emperor. I cannot make a single blunder. Are there any wrinkles in my uniform? Is there any dirt on my shoes? I put on makeup for the first time in a while, but is it natural looking? Did I record today's morning drama? Did I set the timer to record my variety shows?! Do I have my member card for Freshmart Warakia in my wallet?"

"You're getting your regular morning checklist and your meeting-your-sister checklist mixed up."

Shiren was a bundle of nerves first thing in the morning. She had spilled a bit of her miso soup three times already, and the fourth time, it went all over the place. She even tripped over the door when they left.

She's like a girl getting ready to go on a date.

For some reason, Ryouta found himself jealous. But she was just going to see her sister, and even if she were going on a date, his jealousy was his problem. He still had his first crush anyway.

But on the other hand, Ryouta was nervous, too.

He would be asking Shiren's big sister—the Emperor—to absolve Shiren of her crimes.

Frankly speaking, it was hard to tell if it would go well. The worst outcome would be a reply like *Relieve her crimes? No. To the gallows with you, too!* But that probably wouldn't happen. He wanted to believe so anyway.

But if she was praising herself in the contents of their English textbook and all that, there was no doubt she would be the excessively self-conscious type. She was older than Shiren, so she had to be around twenty years old—she was probably extremely proud.

With those thoughts running through his head, they went to school.

"We don't need the chain anymore," Shiren had said, so he only had his collar on. He was getting tired of wearing it, too, but he couldn't take it off if he didn't want the townspeople seriously coming after him.

There was a solemn air all throughout the school.

First of all, the Empire's national flag flew over the school. The design was of a white dragon over a red background. It was cool but also hard to replicate by hand.

"Oh, good morning everyone. This is Tamaki. Today we have our bimonthly inspection by Her Imperial Majesty the Emperor. Will she tell me she is angry with me and sentence me to death? I was so nervous I could barely sleep, and now I worry I will yawn the moment she enters. The idea had me so frightened I couldn't sleep, so now I worry I will yawn the moment she enters. The idea had me so frightened I couldn't sleep, and now I—"

"You're just going in endless circles now, Shijou."

Their other classmates were stiff, too. One of the bubblier guys barely spoke at all. Even the girls in the back who were always chatting stayed in their seats today.

And, as always, no one spoke to Shiren. They didn't hate her—they just didn't know how to treat her, so they stayed away.

He understood how they felt. But in the end, it was still unusual.

But he had always been unusual, and that was why he could do anything.

His position wasn't as sad as hers, but he had always been treated differently because of his spell. He wanted friends, but people put distance between him and them. He couldn't just chat with anybody.

That was why he understood Shiren just a touch more than the other classmates.

If the Emperor offered her relief, then things would change ever so slowly. Shiren wasn't shy at all, so she would probably open up to her class-mates herself. The rest was just a matter of time.

And then his job would be done, and he'd go home to Japan.

In the middle of second period, the time finally came.

A whole mass of footsteps were approaching the classroom. The Emperor obviously wasn't walking around alone—she probably had attendants with her, like Sasara Tatsunami from yesterday.

And then he saw someone wearing a dress stand before the classroom door.

The Emperor of the Sacred Blood Empire would soon enter.

"Okay!" Ryouta whispered to himself and leaped up.

If he moved slowly, they'd catch him and pin him down. At that point, he would be just a simple criminal. He might even be killed.

But this was the only thing he could do.

Victory would go to the one who acted first.

He stood before the door to the classroom and threw himself to the floor.

"Your Imperial Majesty! I may be just a minion, but please listen to my request! Absolve the crimes of my master, Shiren Fuyukura! Your little sister has done nothing wrong, Your Majesty, and I bet you know that, too! As her minion, I guarantee she isn't a bad person! I don't care what happens to me, but please, please give my master, Shiren Fuyukura, the right to walk boldly beneath the sun with a smile on her face!"

He said it. He really said it.

He had been planning on going with the flow with more polite language, but he obviously ended up being more casual than he wanted to. When he forgot to say *please* that one time, he just had to keep going with it.

And after his cry, the class fell completely silent.

It was the casual speech that got him, wasn't it? But otherwise, he didn't think he'd said anything wrong or insulted the Emperor in any way…

He didn't hear anything from the Emperor. Maybe that was why no one could say anything.

Please just respond with anything. These few moments of silence have been too heavy. Or maybe because someone of her exalted standing wasn't to speak directly to people of common birth.

"Wait…"

After a while, he heard her speak.

It was a familiar, high-pitched voice, similar to the one he'd heard from the guard Sasara's stuffed doll.

"Whoa… Don't tell me—is that…you, Ryouta? Ryouta Asagiri?"

Why did she know his name? He hadn't mentioned his last name was Asagiri.

Despite himself, Ryouta looked up to see the Emperor's face.

Standing there was a girl with bright-red hair, clear blue eyes, and a face more overwhelmingly beautiful than anyone else's. Despite the many years they'd spent apart, he recognized her right away.

Sure enough, it was Ryouta's very first love—Ouka Sarano.

"Wait, wait, hold on… You're the Emperor, Ouka?!"

Sasara, her guard, was just about to draw her sword, but Ouka held up a hand to stop her.

"Sasara, it's seems I've been sweating a little. Fix my makeup. Come along!"

"Oh, Your Majesty, why have you taken my hand so? Could this be forbidden love between wome—? Ow, ahhhh! If you pull so suddenly, I will fall over!"

The group was gone in a flurry, like a storm. Fifteen minutes later, Ouka came back with only Sasara in tow.

"Sorry to keep you waiting."

Her makeup was on clearly more neatly than it had been just a moment ago. She had also changed her dress to one with a lot more sparkle.

"Ryouta, I'm sure you have a lot to say, so let us go elsewhere to talk… And you come, too, Shiren."

When Ouka had finished speaking, she left without bothering to confirm with Ryouta.

She didn't even look at Shiren.

"Wait, Ryouta, why do you know the Emperor…?" Shiren asked slowly, shocked.

"Ouka was my classmate in elementary school."

And then Ryouta added:

"And my first crush…"

"Again, it is a pleasure to see you. I am the one hundred seventh emperor of the Sacred Blood Empire, Ouka Elisabeta Alexandra Florentina Sylvia Rosanna Sarano. My first name is correctly written with the characters for 'strike' and 'fire,' but that isn't a very nice name, so please use the characters for 'king' and 'flower' instead. Please make yourselves at home."

They would have loved to, but they were surrounded by furniture that a whole lifetime of earnings could never purchase, so it was hard to relax.

After their earlier exchange, Ryouta and Shiren had been ushered into a long limousine—they had no idea where she would have even bought it—and taken to a castle.

It was a *castle*. On the mountain in the west side of the old city of Akinomiya, an enormous Western-style garrison towered over the rest of the town.

"Ah, we started building this castle three years ago under the pretense that it would be a personal manor. Obviously, we could not have completed it in the months since our country was founded. There were several television reports about an odd house being built, which worried us, but it all worked out in the end. It also has a very safe and reliable anti-earthquake design. As long as Godzilla doesn't step on it, it will never collapse."

"I never imagined you'd be the Emperor, Ouka…"

"It truly has been quite a long time. Seven years, is it? It was right when we were in fourth grade that Papa took the helm of our movement to become independent. People started coming after us, so I ended up transferring suddenly. We then started gradually moving other Sacred Blooded into the Akinomiya area, and so that's how we managed to pull the whole thing off in April of this year. Somebody killed Papa two years ago, though."

Ryouta felt as if he were in a dream—she was telling this unbelievable story so casually.

He thought *he'd* been living a weird life, but this was on a whole other level.

©Hiroki Ozaki

"But I can see you made it this far without knowing I was the Emperor… You didn't come to see me, did you?" Ouka sighed, a slight frown on her face. "You didn't hear my name anywhere? I thought you'd know when you heard the last name Sarano."

"All the textbooks and TV shows just call you the Emperor."

"You never could keep up-to-date on things, could you? Don't tell me you ended up in the Empire because you didn't know that Akinomiya had become our territory or anything like that?"

Bull's-eye.

"And now that I've given you my name as the Emperor, courtesy demands that you give yours! Or I'll hammer a rusted nail under your nails!"

Oh, right, this is the kind of person Ouka is…, Ryouta thought.

"You probably know already, but my name is Ryouta Asagiri— Ow!"

Shiren smacked him from behind. "You're not Ryouta Asagiri! You're Ryouta Fuyukura! Be more conscious of your role as my minion!"

A dark cloud passed over Ouka's expression.

"M-minion…? Her minion…? You still smell a whole lot like a human… Tell me everything that happened! Right now!"

Ryouta told her the story of everything that had occurred in the past ten days. It felt as though it would only get even more complicated if Shiren interjected at any point, so he gave the entire account on his own.

…

"So basically, you came into the country without a single clue as to what was going on; Shiren was the first to find you, then bite you, but you couldn't be completely subjugated, so you were living together at her house, but in the meantime, two others ended up biting you and *kind of* made you their minion, too… I'm impressed—they call me the Iron Woman, and even I'm starting to feel dizzy."

"Your Imperial Majesty, please don't tell me that this dingy boy was your first—"

"Silence." A fan flew at Sasara's head.

"Ouch… But this is the Emperor's lash of love…hnnnng…"

Ouka completely ignored Sasara's reaction and continued with the conversation. "And not only that, but one of those two who bit you was Alfoncina... No matter the season, that woman is always in heat..."

As befitting her status, Ouka addressed the archbishop without her title. But of course, it wasn't like Alfoncina ever acted very important to begin with. Even at school in her uniform, she'd still say unbelievable things like "I hope you're staying healthy. I mean not just normally, but sexually, too."

"And, Shiren, I'm surprised you managed to run into this man. You may be my younger sister, but I still admire your good luck. He was a terrible philanderer back in Japan, if you didn't know."

"Yes, he has told me about it..."

"Hey! Don't drag me like this! You do know that it's out of my control, don't you?!"

He had been insulted so casually, he had to step in. Ouka was ruthless when it came to this stuff.

"It's fine. I bet you're happy you get to chat with girls your age normally, aren't you? They looked at you like meat back at home, after all."

"People here still look at me like I'm meat because I'm Japanese and miraculously still around," he retorted.

Ouka's ears twitched lightly. "There's something I want to check; could we safely call you the sole Japanese person in this country? Demographically, you just might be."

"Probably. But why are you asking me?"

Ouka tapped the fan against her palm like a percussion instrument.

Then she tapped Ryouta's head with it. She was clearly making fun of him.

"I can't believe you're so calm about this. Let's say the sole Japanese person in the Empire gets attacked. Our international reputation will plummet, and it will give the Self-Defense Force a justifiable reason to step in. This means you are an extremely important item! Do you understand?!"

She was right—from the perspective of the head of state, this was a problem she couldn't just overlook.

"I mean, I guess my deal is pretty important, but what about Shiren's problem?"

Still, Ryouta pressed Ouka as if it was the next logical step in the conversation, and he wasn't even trying to be polite this time. The nerves he'd felt earlier had also vanished. It was obvious that if he tried to call her Your Imperial Majesty, she'd just say, *Ew, that's gross; don't say that*—it was Ouka, after all.

Shiren's expression clouded when her name came up.

"I heard your risky appeal loud and clear, Ryouta. I was actually unsure of how to deal with Shiren myself."

Ouka turned to Shiren. Shiren herself seemed very uncomfortable. It had been so long since she had been together with her sister.

"Why do you look like you're going to cry? I'm not going to punish you. The opposite, actually! Be happy! Yay!"

Those sounded like Ouka-style words of encouragement to Ryouta.

"Well, I'll need to get rid of what's troubling you, won't I? Shiren, I will absolve you of your crimes, and you will come to the palace officially as the Emperor's younger sister. You will also take the name of Sarano, which is only allowed for the members of the Imperial family."

At that moment, Shiren's face opened up into a grin, like a flower of joy blooming on her face.

"Th-thank you so much, Your Majesty!" Shiren fell to her knees.

"No need to be so dramatic. I wanted you to live in the palace right away, you know. The reason I've been visiting the school every once in a while was to prepare for this. But without some sort of catalyst, the national sentiment would not readily shift in favor. That was why it was perfect that Ryouta said what he did when he did. I'll just play the part of 'kind emperor whose heart was swayed by a loyal minion.'"

"I dunno, that's bad taste."

"It's politics. Dark rumors were also starting to circulate, you see, and I wanted to do something as quickly as possible. There was word of fundamentalists after Shiren's life."

Ryouta was sick of this. Why did people do these things, even when the Emperor herself didn't want that to happen?

"What a nuisance, isn't it? Well, it will never be more than a rumor, but just in case, it would be better to live within the castle. We'll start getting you ready for the move, let's say…tomorrow."

The conversation pressed onward, as if all their worries from earlier were just a dream.

"Oh no, Ryouta! We need to go home right away and start packing! Be sure to take out *Eden of Pleasure* from beneath your blanket!"

"I'm not hiding anything! And why is all the porn in this country *Eden of Pleasure*?!"

Was Tamaki selling less-than-legal goods out of the Fuyukura house? He'd have to double-check later.

"Man, living in a castle, though. Hard to imagine."

He hadn't even dreamed of such a drastic change to their modest living situation.

"Of course, that means all the cleaning, cooking, and laundry will be your job at the castle as well, Ryouta. You must obey the orders of the Emperor's younger sister with more loyalty than you ever have! You will commit yourself to me! Oh-ho!"

When Ryouta saw Shiren's high spirits, he felt a twinge of fear, knowing he'd be worked into the ground.

If I really end up living like a butler in a huge mansion, I'm gonna burn out before long…

"Hold on, Shiren. Listen to everything I need to say."

There was a chill in Ouka's voice that froze Shiren in place.

"You will be living in the castle, Shiren. As for you, Ryouta, the direct appeal made today is considered a crime of lèse-majesté. As punishment, you will be stripped from your position as Shiren's minion. A minion's sins are his master's. I mean, you weren't even officially her minion in the first place."

""What?""

Ryouta and Shiren inadvertently spoke as one.

"But that means Ryouta is without a place to stay, so…so you will be my minion. A minion under direct service of the Emperor. Be… Be thankful. This is all because we have no other choice, do you hear me? This means I'll have to drink your blood… But this is the only thing we can do. As long as I keep my composure, everything will turn out fine…"

"Hey, what on Earth are you talking about, Ouka?"

"What I'm saying is not strange at all. As a Japanese person who wandered into our country, you must be received appropriately. This is consistent with the Empire's national policy. You were almost subjugated twice in the ten days you were with Shiren, correct? We can't leave you out in such a place. You might be her minion candidate, but the claim is still unreliable. In which case, you just need to start off as my minion, the Emperor's minion. I highly doubt anyone is audacious enough to try to steal a minion from the Emperor, and the Emperor's minions automatically receive a title and earn a place among the nobility. I'm sure the people of Japan wouldn't think terribly of you if they found out a Japanese citizen had been made a noble in another country. Knowing your blood was sucked might affect your reputation negatively, but considering the risks of staying as a pure Japanese person, it's a fantastic bargain. There's also the rumors of those ultranationalists after Shiren's life. It would never happen, but if you were to be killed because you were her minion, that would put the entire Empire in an awkward position, internationally. And so that is why you should live with us as my minion. Well, my logic is perfect, if I do say so myself."

Her reasons might all be correct, but…

"I mean, sure, but I can't just do it out of the blue…"

"I'm sorry, Ryouta, but you are in such a unique position that you cannot live freely in this country. And I thought I said this a long time ago…that I would protect you," Ouka said, her face slightly flushed, her gaze averted. "I was just a powerless elementary school girl back then, but I'm not now. With the authority I have now, I can make any wish you have come true. I can put an end to your days as prey. I doubt you have any reason to refuse," she explained. "Or does the idea of becoming my minion really repulse you that much?"

"Well, that's not what I mea—"

"I cannot allow this!"

Suddenly, someone intervened—Sasara, the Imperial guard.

"What is the meaning of this, making more minions?! I stand in firm opposition to your subjugating this nondescript, horse manure–like human! Not to mention he's a *boy*! You must stay as pure white and unsullied as snow, Your Imperial Majesty!"

"Hold on! You could at least be a little nicer about it! Why manure?!"

"Why *not* manure?! The horse-dung sea urchin is an exquisitely high-quality ingredient!"

"No, you were definitely using it to insult me!"

"But of course! You will not approach Her Impe— *Guh!*"

Ouka smacked her fan on the crown of Sasara's head. "You, be quiet. I am speaking to Ryouta. You will be given the ax. And I mean that quite literally." She really didn't mean it in the metaphorical sense. Sasara fell silent in fear.

"What I'm saying is, since Shiren and I live together, I can't just leave her alone—"

"No, it's fine. Thanks for everything you've done for me so far." Shiren patted him lightly on the shoulder. "It's all exactly as the Emperor says. The longer you stay with me, the more danger that puts you in, Ryouta. I can't ask you to do that."

"I know it makes sense, but…"

Ryouta was bewildered to see Shiren giving in so easily.

You can't ask me to do something? That's not like you at all.

Despite how outrageously she'd been acting, she seemed way too pleased with this arrangement.

"We're going to start living separately tomorrow on. Are you okay with that?"

"I won't be alone anymore." Shiren's expression seemed incredibly mature, but also slightly sad. "There are no crimes to my name. I can start making friends now. If I relied on you forever, I'd just stay the same, wouldn't I?"

"Yeah, I get it, but—"

"Your service ends today."

With one short sentence, it felt as if his connection with Shiren had been cleanly severed.

Judging just from the situation, Ryouta shouldn't have any counter-arguments. The whole reason he tried to go back to Japan was to see Ouka, and he'd managed to complete his goal in the end. Not only that, but he would become Ouka's minion.

But he still wasn't satisfied with this. It felt like he was making a big mistake.

When Ouka saw the expression on his face, she took down a large sword that was hanging on the wall.

"Take this sword, Ryouta."

She held it out to him. The sword was shivering—Ouka's hands were shaking.

"Wait, I can have this…?"

"Just take it, quickly! I've never held something as heavy as this!"

With no other choice, Ryouta took the sword. It was just as heavy as its large size suggested.

"What?! He took the Royal Sword… But that's supposed to be the symbol of the Imperial Guard!" Sasara cried. "This means the likes of a human will be joining the ranks of the Guard! This is unheard-of!"

"Wait, wait, what? I didn't know this! Hey!"

But Ouka didn't seem bothered at all by Ryouta's bewilderment.

"All the Emperor's minions are obligated to protect her when the time calls for it. This sword is the symbol of that idea. You will protect me with all the strength you can muster. Oh, and the Emperor's orders are absolute, okay? You can hate me as much as you want. And as long as I don't find out, you can do as many naughty things to me in your mind as you want. Being in this job, I've gotten used to people hating me. Gosh, it is a crime to be this beautiful," Ouka added with a straight face.

Neither Ryouta nor Shiren had the power to erase this whole conversation from history. They couldn't even put together an argument that made sense.

"Well then, you shall hear the details from me in due course. I can't separate you so suddenly right now, so both of you go home together. Wait in front of the gates, and the car will come for you."

They both had a bad taste left in their mouths; neither of them could say anything.

If only the car would come faster.

But before it could, Sasara came rushing toward them.

"I made it! Here is a personal letter from Her Imperial Majesty. It seems she has something to tell you two." She held a sealed letter in her hands. "By the way, I have not opened it to read the inside or anything like that."

"If you have to tell us, it sounds more like you did…"

"She found out I did that once, and she almost gave me the ax for real. Literally."

"Please just retire."

"Anyway, I've handed it over now! Please be sure not to lose it, so read it when you return home!"

And then the long limousine finally came.

They returned home and opened the letter.

With delicate, careful writing, it said the following:

Shiren & Ryouta Fuyukura,

I am so sorry for causing so much chaos. It was all very sudden. However, I had no other choice but to do so. I believe this is the most peaceable way to settle things.

If it is all right with you, I would like you to come once again to the castle tonight after eight PM, to the back garden. It won't be too extravagant, but I want to have a party with you two. Also, since Sasara and the other guards were nearby, there were some things I wasn't able to talk to you about. I could give you a call, but the phones might be bugged. If you show the guards at the rear garden the sword I gave you, they will let you through right away.

I will be waiting.

Ouka Elisabeta Alexandra Florentina Sylvia Rosanna Sarano

"We should at least part with a smile, Ryouta."

Shiren's expression looked like a smile on the surface. But—

Your eyes aren't smiling at all…

Hiding her feelings was too advanced for Shiren. Ryouta knew that well. But at that moment, he couldn't point it out to her.

"Yeah. And it doesn't seem like there's any way for us to tell her no."

He was hoping to put his all into making his last dinner with Shiren, but if Ouka was going to prepare a feast for them, that was still a relief for him.

"Ryouta, I was really happy with what happened today." Shiren produced a key and slipped it into the keyhole on his collar. "When you faced the Emperor and put your life on the line to say that, it meant so much to me. I would have cried if there weren't anyone else in the classroom. This story might end up in the morals textbook next year. You are the best, the most authentic minion—I'm proud to have been your master. That's why you don't need this collar anymore."

Shiren took the loosened collar and tossed it into a corner of the room.

Two feelings welled up in his chest at the same time—relief at being freed from his shackle, and loss from their breaking connection.

"On top of that, I can openly call myself Sarano as the Emperor's little sister. That last name is only something the Imperial family can use."

"It sure is an unusual name."

"The character for 'blood' can be broken down into two smaller characters: the kanji of *sara* and the katakana *no*, you see. We just made up some kanji to go with it. And so *blood* itself is the perfect last name for the family that governs the Sacred Blooded."

The majestic resonance of the name was certainly suited for an emperor's bloodline.

"This has been the happiest day of my life. I finally understand that the Emperor has been thinking of me this entire time. We *are* sisters, after all."

Ryouta was also relieved that Shiren's big sister was Ouka; he knew she would look after her little sister. She'd always seemed like the type to fuss over other people.

But even though Shiren said she was happy, that sentiment didn't appear on her face at all. Shiren wasn't addressing Ouka as a sister—she was still calling her the Emperor.

"That's right; you're being promoted."

"So are you. The Emperor's minions might be considered servants, but in reality, they are very close to her, and they're treated as nobles, status-wise. So be happy! You don't have to look so awkward!"

Shiren slapped him several times on the back.

"Did I look awkward...?"

"Really, Ryouta, you look like you're in pain! We aren't going to be apart forever! Be happier like the clueless child you are—you're leaving Shiren Fuyukura's side to join the Emperor as her minion! If you don't, I'll...I'll just end up sad, too..."

She gave a small sigh to wipe her feelings away. She was right—nobody would end up happy if they dwelled on it anymore.

"All right. Then we'll make tonight's party one to remember." He ruffled Shiren's hair.

"Exactly, that's what I'm— Hey, how rude can you be toward your master?!"

She punched him straight in the sternum. "*Guh...* You can't immediately resort to violence like that... I'm going to report this to the UN's Human Rights Commission..."

"It is a lash of love toward one's minion. Don't forget it. You are only my minion for another few hours. I will expect no less than perfect service." Shiren rested her hand gently on Ryouta's back one more time. "For another few hours yet, you are not the Emperor's. You are mine."

"Yeah. I'm still your minion."

Only for the few hours until the date changed.

"Hey, Ryouta, could you let me drink your blood one last time?"

Ryouta leaned forward a little; Shiren was too short to get a good bite on his neck. "As you wish, Master." Even if she wasn't his master, he'd still let her drink as much blood of his as she wanted. Once he became the Emperor's minion, it would probably be illegal. For Shiren or anyone else.

Then would this be the last time?

But if this completely turned him into Shiren's minion, what would happen to him?

The Emperor probably didn't have the right to nullify a contractual relationship that had already been established.

"Here goes— *Nom.*"

He was starting to get used to the pain in his neck. The part she was biting into slowly felt as if it were being encased in ice. And then a spot of blood started oozing out.

"*Sigh...* Your blood is strange, Ryouta. I don't know why I can taste a mix of so many flavors from it. It really warms me up."

"I don't know if I'm happy to be complimented for my blood, but sure. Thanks."

He wrapped his empty arms around Shiren's back. He wanted to feel a bit closer to her, since this would be the last time.

In the end, Shiren slowly licked the wound she left behind by her bite twice.

"Okay, Ryouta, spin around three times and say in a loud voice, *I am Lady Shiren's minion.*"

"Huh? Why do I need to act like an idiot?"

For a moment, he didn't get it, but after a quick think, he remembered this check was in that book, *My First Minion...*

"...Oh! Uhhh, spin three times—"

As he was about to spin around, Shiren grabbed his hands to stop him.

"Don't force yourself. It's like I thought—I don't have the power to make my own minions. I finally realize that. It's not that I was maturing slowly, and it's not because I'm a child. My power to make minions is weak because I'm half human. That's all."

A mature, mirthless smile rested on Shiren's face.

"You really were lucky I was the one who picked you up, Ryouta!" She showed him another smile this time, one she had probably worked hard to summon.

"Yeah, I really was."

"Oh, right, we haven't had lunch yet. Let's go to the neighborhood soba shop! My treat!"

"If it has blood in it, then no thanks."

"Okay, then we'll eat in."

"Wait, so it *did* have blood in it?!"

The clock in the room was pointing to a little past one.

The party was on in just under seven hours.

EPISODE 5
LET'S SEIZE POWER IN THE EMPIRE!

"Hey, Ryouta, how do I look in this dress?"

"I guess it doesn't look too bad— Whoa! There's no back! Pick one that shows less skin!"

"What, are you jealous?"

"I'm not gonna feel that way no matter how you slice it, so no. Don't worry."

It seemed there was plenty of time until the party, but there really wasn't.

Their host was the Emperor, after all. It would be embarrassing if they just showed up in normal clothes. It was also an event that would be marking a turning point in Shiren's life, so she had to be dressed well for it.

And that was why they'd come to a boutique near the station (which was still there, even though the trains didn't run anymore).

"I enjoyed your reaction. I'm picking this one."

"Do what you want. It's your money."

"Next I just need something on my neck with bones, like the archbishop had—"

"That'll just turn you into a shaman. Wait, do Sacred Blooded really wear bones? Like, is that part of your aesthetic?"

"No, that's just the archbishop's style. We lived as Japanese citizens for a long time, so our tastes don't differ too much from theirs. And she herself said she was creating a character for herself."

"She could be religious her whole life, but she probably wouldn't be able to get into heaven…"

"You look good in a suit, too, Ryouta. You look like a CEO who takes the last train home every day."

"That's a dark future to look forward to! But thanks, I guess."

Ryouta decided he may as well get a suit since the occasion was calling for it. Showing up in his school uniform would just be sloppy.

Beside him was a sword that looked a little out of place. It was a symbol of his position as a swordsman serving the Emperor directly.

Quite a number of people had looked at him, impressed, before they reached the area around the station.

As he killed time browsing the sale racks, Shiren came back from the register, still in her dress. She had apparently finished paying for it.

"Well, now that we still have time until the party…"

She tugged lightly on the sleeve of his suit. She was much gentler than she had been with his collar.

"Ryouta… Since we're already here and dressed up, why don't we go somewhere nearby? There's a nice terrace café here."

Almost a whole third of the seating at this place was outside, which gave it a nice atmosphere. But because of that, it was about three times as expensive as a chain café.

A small river flowed by, and there were even fish swimming in it.

"Wow! I can taste the original essence of the beans from the coffee! I suppose this is the highest quality coffee house in the whole Empire. I shall give it my highest compliments!"

"You sure are acting all high and mighty for someone who hasn't been officially recognized as the Emperor's little sister yet."

"Oh, not at all. This is a famous café frequented by the noble class—those with power within the Empire, I mean. They are extremely careful not to use a single drop of blood in their brews so that their patrons may enjoy the taste of the coffee itself."

"Wait, you mean all the other shops use blood…? Hello?"

"In the Emperor's book, *The Beautiful Young Emperor's Foodie Journey of the Empire* (Sacred Blood Empire Publishing), she gave it a whole three stars."

"I'm kind of impressed Ouka has the nerve to call herself beautiful like that so openly. But you're saying the other shops have blood in their coffee? Right?"

"I would love to come to a shop like this with the Emperor one day."

"I'm really sorry for trying to wrap up your conversation about this very nice thing, but can you please tell me more about this blood stuff? Seriously!"

"Hey, what do you think the biggest difference between demons and Satan is?"

"Quit blatantly changing the subject!"

He suspected that if he didn't get a clear answer out of her right then, he never would.

"It's fine. *(whisper, whisper)*"

"Why did you have to say that so quietly…?"

It sounded like he wasn't supposed to touch on this subject.

Two women came out to the terrace, but when they spotted Shiren and Ryouta, they started murmuring to each other ("Oh, there's a couple out here." "Let's go inside. We shouldn't bother them.") and went back inside.

Shiren had apparently heard it loud and clear, as her ears were bright red.

"Well, I guess that's what people would think when they see two high schoolers at such a fancy café," Ryouta offered a word. Things would only get more awkward if he stayed silent.

"Y-you're right… We aren't equals anyway; we have a hierarchical relationship. Master and servant."

"But that'll be over in a few hours, though."

"Which means after that, we'll be able to enter a more equal relationship, right…?"

Had Shiren's face gotten closer?

"Oh, yeah, I think you're right…"

It made sense. In due time, neither would be considered superior.

"S-so when we do become equals, do you want to come back to this café?" Shiren's voice was a little strained.

"Sure. It might be a nice way to celebrate…" Ryouta also gave his consent. They would reunite wearing fancy clothes, as people who'd made it in the world.

The Emperor's younger sister and the Emperor's personal guard, alone together. That wasn't a bad combination, was it?

"Well, of course! We should come every day! Since I'll be officially the Emperor's little sister, I could probably get into any place I want for free!"

"Don't do that! The people will hate you! You're thinking like a cheapskate!"

"Then I'll list it as expenses. In the Empire's special account."

"That's a waste of taxpayer money!"

Times like this, it was easy to see the two sisters were related.

"Okay, then we'll meet here at the same table! We'll take turns reminiscing on all our joy and sorrow. Like how great your master was back then, and how beautiful she was, and how smart she was!"

"Oh, so we're only going to talk about your brilliant success. Okay."

"We could also talk about your devoted service, if you want to." Shiren smiled and held out her right hand.

"What, are we shaking hands?"

"It's a pinkie promise. It means we'll meet again one day."

"If you say so."

Ryouta held out his hand. Just this simple ritual of intertwining pinkie with pinkie had a stronger power than any contract they could produce now.

But just before their fingers met, Shiren pulled back her hand and shook her head sadly.

"We can't dwell on the past forever. A new future is waiting for us."

"Yeah, you're right."

The breeze that passed over the terrace was chillier than he'd expected. He was cold.

"Then I guess it's almost time to go. We need to give ourselves plenty of time. Ouka hates waiting for people."

The perimeter of the castle was, of course, surrounded by guards, but Ryouta showed the sword to the one in the back.

"Oh! Please go right through!"

All the nearby soldiers bowed to him with the utmost respect, too.

"Incredible! It's like a skeleton key for people. Ryouta, let's see how high up the hierarchy that'll work tomorrow."

"You're awful. It's in the back garden, so is it over this way?"

"The Emperor's party… I bet there'll be some kind of surprise. Like eating food off a naked lady."

"Are you an old man? Yikes, I can imagine her pulling something like that… I just hope there isn't anything that ruins the mood…"

Shiren linked her arm with Ryouta's. "Today's the only day we can do things like this. You will obey your master, even if you're embarrassed."

There was a hint of mischief in Shiren's smile. That wasn't an expression he'd seen on her before.

"As you wish."

As he looked at her, he ruminated on what he would say to Ouka when he saw her.

There were tables set out throughout the back garden, but Ouka was nowhere to be seen yet. She was probably busy with official affairs, or maybe she just hadn't shown up because it wasn't time yet.

There was still time for them to talk on their own.

"Hey, Shiren, just pretend what you hear next is a humble minion talking to himself."

"Um, sure, okay. What is it?"

"Shiren, what if I get tired of life in the palace and stuff? What if I decide I don't belong here anymore?"

"Mm-hmm."

"If that happens, then we should escape across the mountain back to Japan together. We'd probably have a great time living together."

"I know you said this is a monologue, but let me interject. Why do I have to run away? I've never thought about such a thing, not even once."

"Then why were you right by the mountain on the day you bit me? You weren't out shopping, were you? You weren't going on a picnic empty-handed or anything, right?"

He saw something in Shiren's face change.

"And it's not like your neighborhood is near the mountain or anything.

There's nothing else there, and you wouldn't have had any friends to hang out with on the weekends. So since I'm just monologuing, let me speak my mind—maybe Shiren wanted to escape from the Empire, and that's why she was near the mountain?"

Shiren was, unmistakably, the Emperor's younger sister. Despite who her mother may have been, she was still a direct descendant of the Imperial line, and not somebody Ryouta should be speaking so casually with.

But that and whether she actually enjoyed being the Emperor's little sister were two completely separate questions. Not only that, a portion of the population labeled her and treated her as a rebel; she had become so lonely that she was thinking about defecting or running away. That wasn't a normal situation.

"I know I told you this before, but Ouka was my first crush. On the other hand, that doesn't mean I have to always spend time with her, and if, and I really mean *if*, there was a possibility I ended up falling in love with y—"

And then something leaped out at them from the grass, grabbed Shiren, and peeled her away from Ryouta.

It happened in an instant. Ryouta couldn't even step in the way to cover Shiren.

But the intervention of an amateur like him wouldn't have made a difference anyway.

That *something* was, without a doubt, a member of the Virginal Father—Kiyomizu Jouryuuji.

"You have gotten much too close to my dearest Ryouta, little Sacred Blooded dog. Step away from him, if you please. Preferably forever."

Shiren was pinned to the grass.

Kiyomizu was holding her with an unbelievable amount of strength for her slender body. She also wore a Sacred Blooded battle uniform.

"Why are you here, Kiyomizu?! This isn't the border; this is the Emperor's castle! What happened to security here?!"

"You're up against me," said a fourth person.

Suddenly, Ryouta felt someone coming for him with deadly purpose, just like on the field trip, and he swiftly blocked the incoming swing of an enemy sword with the sheath of his own.

The one who had attacked him was the Imperial guard Sasara.

"What are you doing…?"

"My job is to keep the Emperor's peace and order. You are a Japanese person who has only just left his home country and is not a total, official minion yet. I cannot allow you to get anywhere near the Emperor, can I?" Though her initial surprise attack failed, Sasara didn't seem upset at all as she stepped back to put space between them. "That is especially true for someone hanging around an assassination target."

"Wait, don't tell me you're going to…"

He'd heard there were people after Shiren's life, but he didn't think someone so close to the Emperor was involved.

"Indeed—if you think about it, you shouldn't be surprised. If the Emperor's little sister stays alive, it's entirely possible she may be used to drag the emperor down from power. Especially so if half her blood is human."

Interesting. The whole idea wasn't that far out there.

But it took him way too long to realize the party itself was a trap!

"And that is why I, a member of the Virginal Father, am here," Kiyomizu finished. "Didn't you think it odd that there were no officers around the border in the mountain?"

That solved the mystery.

"You called Kiyomizu out to kill Shiren?" he asked.

It wasn't a coincidence he'd run into Kiyomizu in the mountain. Sasara had called her and hoped Shiren would head there herself.

"I was there as well," Sasara replied. "That was because I was hoping to remove you from the equation, too, but I gave up because you ended up running into that Virginal Father girl first."

That menacing aura he'd felt when he went into the mountain wasn't Kiyomizu, but Sasara.

"It's not so bad if she manages to kill someone in the Emperor's direct line, is it?" said Sasara. "I would also be grateful if she took care of such adulterous blood. We must fight fire with fire, you see."

"She is exactly right, my dearest and most noble Ryouta. I will soon make a bloodfest out of this deceitful witch," Kiyomizu said lightly, but she was fully intending to kill.

"This doesn't help anyone... Why...?" This whole ridiculous reality was starting to irritate Ryouta. He couldn't believe he had to worry about dying before he even got the chance to worry about being apart from Shiren. "First, there's no way you're actually working together, right? Kiyomizu, you do know you're in cahoots with someone trying to kill me?"

"I made a promise with her that she would only half kill you, at most, Ryouta dear. And afterward, I can do as I please with you. That is why I will be taking you back to my room in Japan."

"Wait, I get why Japan, but why does it have to be your house? To your room, specifically...?"

He could feel his blood draining just by imagining what would happen there.

"I have one hundred and eight secret tools made to please you in my room."

He was terrified by the idea that she might be telling the truth...

"Your death would be ideal, of course, but if that happened, I would only end up in battle against this creepy little Virginal Father girl."

"Have you looked in the mirror? Your love for Ouka is just as creepy..."

"My love for Her Imperial Majesty is pure and perfectly acceptable. Oh, by the way, I almost fainted today just watching my emperor, delicate as a lily blossom, speaking with a filthy male like you. I will one day amend the law to exile all men from this country."

"Ouka, please just exile this guard already!"

"Really, I wish to rid the world of all those who offend Her Imperial Majesty, male or otherwise. That is why this woman, the Emperor's sister, is in the way."

It didn't sound as if she was an ultranationalist or anything like that—just a lesbian with an unhealthy obsession.

The problem was that she was a swordswoman in direct service to the Emperor.

"How long do you plan to keep me pinned to the ground, you insolent fool?! I am the Emperor's younger sister!"

While Kiyomizu was distracted, Shiren took her chance to escape from under her.

But Ryouta and Shiren were up against an assassin and an Imperial guard—they weren't escaping that easily. The two would be killed the second they turned their backs.

"Now we put an end to this long conversation! I will cut you for every word you spoke to the Emperor!"

"That won't make me half-dead—that'll make me dead-dead!"

Ryouta blocked Sasara's blade with the sword he had been granted. What would've happened to them if he didn't have this?

"Ryouta! Give me three minutes, and I'll pummel these petty underlings! So just hang on for three minutes!" He heard Shiren's voice from behind him.

"I thought you weren't a good athlete?!"

"Beating up villains is my specialty. Three minutes, hang in there for three minutes!"

Hang in there? No way—but still, he had to. If anything, he needed to defeat Sasara and go help Shiren in three minutes.

If he didn't, then Shiren—his master—would die.

"Dammit! Come at me, Sasara!"

He blocked all of Sasara's attacks for now. There was nothing else he could do.

Each time their blades crossed, he was met with an overwhelming wave of force. He'd be impressed by the prowess of this Imperial guard if he had the energy for it.

But he was only barely defending himself.

"What, do you have a few swordsmanship skills under your belt? This is the first time an amateur has fended off my attacks for more than ten seconds."

"I've been attacked by girls from the kendo club more than just once or twice! I've literally lived through the Warriors games. That's why I know at least a few things about self-defense!"

The tragic events of his past replayed like a kaleidoscope in his mind.

...*Stop—kaleidoscopes are bad luck.*

But he couldn't believe his terrible past would be helping him now—he truly was unfortunate. If only he could have had a peaceful life where he would never have had to learn these things.

©Hiroki Ozaki

"Shiren! Stay put for just three minutes! I'll give this obsessive swords-woman a good beating! This is for Ouka's honor, too!"

"Heh, I'll be giving this obsessive ninja a good beating in the next three minutes as well!"

He wasn't really sure if he'd call Kiyomizu a ninja, but the knives she was throwing at Shiren did look a lot like *kunai*.

Shiren deftly avoided them.

Over and over again.

Even when Kiyomizu got behind her.

"—Wait, Shiren, you don't have any weapons or anything, do you…?"

"I was thinking about picking up the weapons this girl is throwing at me and throwing them back. No good?"

"You think you can win by treating this like an old action game?!"

This was bad, and it would only get worse if he didn't put Sasara in the ground, fast.

"One stab from this, and you're done for."

From her toolbox, Kiyomizu whipped out a spear that was about eight feet long. Definitely longer than her box.

"How on Earth did you fit that in there?!" Shiren interjected in surprise.

"This is my Loooooooong Spear, one of my secret weapons. It's perfect for skewering worms that deceive you, Ryouta. Right now they're on sale; buy one, get one free!"

"You need *two*?! Why are you selling them?!"

This was bad. Shiren was already at a disadvantage, and now Kiyomizu was far better equipped.

"You can do it, Shiren. Don't die!"

"Am I so little of a threat? Worry about yourself!" Sasara's blade sliced his arm.

In retrospect, the amount of blood Shiren drew when she bit him was almost nothing compared with how much was gushing from his arm.

"I was impatient at first, but I see you were simply a novice who learned to spar by watching others—nothing. Once I learned your pattern, it was over for you."

He had his limits. He'd never taken real lessons.

And even if he did have experience, it was still unlikely he'd be able to contend with a pro.

"I said I'd only half kill you, didn't I? So how is this?"

This time she sliced his thigh. His shoulder. His back. The number of cuts on his body slowly grew.

His vision turned red—she must have cut his forehead.

Yeesh, RPG status ailments are more realistic than I thought.

His ability to concentrate was slipping so much that his mind was wandering to irrelevant topics.

"This…is too much…" He unwittingly whimpered. "They're way out of line, and they believe they're right… But without the power to prove it…"

Even if Sasara said she would stop before he died, his body was still screaming of the danger from all those wounds. He couldn't think about anything else.

Then he heard Shiren scream.

He saw a hazy image of blood spilling from her arm.

"Shiren!"

The danger his life was in, and the fear that came with it, vanished. His life was hardly worth anything anyway.

"O-ouch! Ouch!"

"Oh? That wasn't enough to kill you. I intend to pierce your heart this time. If I had a say, though, I would prefer if Ryouta pierced me. Sexually."

What the hell led her to believe this was a time for inappropriate jokes?

But either way, an unarmed character had no chance against a character with a weapon!

What could he do to stop this? What could Ryouta Fuyukura do?

"The screams of a worm do nothing but hurt my ears, so I'll ease your pain in one blow. You may beg for your life, if you wish. I'll still kill you, though."

There was nothing he could do. When it came to pure athletic ability, Shiren could be a good match for Kiyomizu, but without a weapon, then…

—Weapon?

"Idiot! You have a weapon right here!" He tossed his sword to her. "Take it, Shiren! Hold on to it with your life!"

Shiren caught it gracefully—and just barely managed to deflect Kiyomizu's attack.

"Th-thank you…Ryouta. You saved me…" Shiren gripped the sword, her eyes wide and blank. "Huh? But, Ryouta, don't you have anything else…?"

He opened up his arms wide.

"Nothing, obviously."

"What are you even thinking? This is absurd!"

The first one to make any comment about Ryouta's actions was Sasara.

"Absurd? You're Ouka's minion, aren't you? Isn't this something a minion would do?" Ryouta shot back with shameless confidence. "You asked me earlier how I could think about other people, right? Shiren isn't just *other people*—she's my master. It's a minion's job to think about their master before anything else."

For a brief second, Sasara went pale. "Are you really fighting for your master now?"

Then her complexion turned a boiling red.

"You will go to hell for that pride of yours. I will cut you to the brink of death."

"Fine. I'll run for thirty seconds. In just thirty seconds, Shiren will defeat Kiyomizu, and she'll come back me up. Isn't that right, Master?"

Surprise passed over Shiren's face at the question, but it was quickly replaced by a smile. "Yes, of course. But you will wait only fifteen seconds, Ryouta!"

"You will not last that long!"

He dodged Sasara's attacks with all he could. He was more used to running than fighting, so he would just stay away from her for now.

"I don't know if I can allow you to take Ryouta's weapon. I will kill you now, worm."

"Try me, loser."

The spear and sword faced each other to deal the finishing blow with a terrible clash of metal against metal that sent both weapons flying through the air.

Shiren closed the distance between her and Kiyomizu, as though she had anticipated this.

"You were planning on knocking the weapons away from the start!"

"I was. Because I know I can win in close quarters—with my fists."

"Hmph, even I know the basics of hand-to-hand—"

"If you stay still for just ten seconds, I'll allow you the rights to **** Ryouta for a whole day."

For a moment, the air around them froze.

Then Kiyomizu's malice vanished. "R... R... R-r-r-r-r-r-r-r-r-r-r-really?!"

"I am Ryouta's master. I will not lie. Just as I said, you may do what you wish with him for a full day, for twenty-four hours. Give him a lifetime's worth of wooing. So just for ten seconds, stay—"

"Okay." She responded at the speed of light. Negotiations had concluded.

She couldn't have thought it through and responded that fast... She just went on instinct...

"Take this as our written agreement! Don't take this personally!"

Now that Kiyomizu had closed her eyes and stopped resisting, Shiren gave her a clean uppercut.

Even as she soared through the air, Kiyomizu was grinning.

"I won, Ryouta!"

"What have you done...?"

"You can't make an omelet without breaking a few eggs!" Shiren called. "Just forget about it!"

It felt as if he'd taken out a loan of five hundred thousand yen just to pay off a debt of the same amount...

And on top of that, it turned the tables in their favor for only a moment.

"I've changed my mind."

As he concentrated on the tip of the sword, Sasara's feet suddenly moved—and by the time that movement finally registered, she had already kicked him into the air. He tumbled awkwardly across the ground, as if he'd been hit by a car.

"I will be putting my fight with you on hold for a moment," Sasara said, then turned her gaze straight to Shiren. "I hope you do not mind fighting with me next?"

"I was just about to ask myself! …But I don't have my sword back yet…"

"Don't waste your breath!"

And once again, Shiren was being attacked, unarmed.

And Sasara was barely breaking a sweat.

Little by little, Shiren was gaining wounds.

"Her Imperial Majesty is trying to create a country for the Sacred Blooded alone. Impurities like you are a nuisance. You will only weaken our union."

"Hmph, you are just an insignificant ultranationalist. It seems you do not clearly understand the Emperor's ideals. She's aiming to create a nation strong enough for anything, including 'impurities'!"

"I know that! But when you appear, the Emperor spends less time looking at me! Her little sister and childhood friend may exit stage right!"

This whole thing wasn't about logic to begin with. This Sasara girl really just couldn't see or think about anyone besides Ouka.

Meaning they had no choice but to stop her by force.

Ryouta stepped toward one of the dropped weapons to pick it up when—

"Shi…ren…"

—he collapsed.

His exhaustion and blood loss had sapped the strength from his body. He was still bleeding—in the present continuous tense—from several places.

"This is just pathetic…"

He hated that he collapsed just as his master was about to be killed. It was an awful way to end his last day as Shiren's minion.

"Dammit… If I'm bleeding this much, then I at least want Shiren to drink it all…! Shiren, drink me dry; turn me into a mummy!"

But he was unsure if those words ever made it out of his mouth.

"Ryouta! Are you okay?!" He heard her voice faintly. Oh no, his consciousness was about to go dark.

"You don't have time to worry about others!" Sasara shouted. She ignored the fading Ryouta and went straight for Shiren.

He was completely out of the equation. They weren't even paying attention to him.

Could he stand to let them underestimate him like this?

He was a proud minion.

He mustered all the strength he had left to stand, and he ran.

Until he was standing in Sasara's way.

"I won't let you…"

It was a miracle he could get to his feet at all. But he had to act for Shiren's sake, even if that meant he wouldn't be moving for the next week, the next month.

"It would have been wiser to remain on the ground."

She didn't even go after him with her sword. She simply kicked him away, and that was enough to send him sailing through the air like a ball.

"I apologize for the interruption, but I will now— *Tch.*"

Sasara clicked her tongue—Ryouta had stood up again. "I'm practically a ghost now, aren't I…?" He wasn't sure what laws of the universe were letting him still move around, but he placed himself between Shiren and Sasara. He wouldn't let Sasara pass, not even over his dead body.

"Just stop it already, Ryouta! That'll only buy us a few seconds. It won't help!"

He heard Shiren's cry loud and clear.

"It won't help? Lying on the ground won't help. If a minion can't save his master, then he's completely worthless!"

I'm still your minion.

"Then I shall do exactly as you wish." Once again, Sasara kicked him away.

This time, he landed right next to Shiren.

"Shi…ren…"

"Ryouta!"

They gazed into each other's eyes—it felt like some kind of a bad joke, since it truly seemed this would be their last chance.

"I will take it upon myself to cut down both master and servant with one strike. That way, neither of you will need to be sad. Isn't that right?"

"But I mean, there's no point if I can't keep my master safe…"

Standing up again was impossible now. If only he could put something else there to stop her—

"Enough, now." Shiren's warm hand settled on his shoulder.

"No, it's *not* enough! Don't give up! We'll manage if we can just figure out a way to knock her down!"

"Who said I was giving up?"

Shiren's voice was filled with hope, courage, and conviction.

"It is now my turn to save you, Ryouta." Shiren immediately grasped Ryouta's arm. His bloodied arm.

"How...sure are you that you'll win...?"

"One hundred percent. I mean, look at how much you're bleeding."

"You're not lying to me, right?"

"No. All the time you bought me allowed me to come up with a plan. I'll show you what comes of paying close attention in class."

Shiren began licking the blood spilling from Ryouta's arm.

Carefully.

Seductively, even, as befitting someone with Sacred Blood.

When people imagined someone drinking blood, it was this.

"Why this now...?"

"We learned this in health class at school, remember? What happens when you lick the blood of someone you love?"

There was a sudden gleam of light in Ryouta's fading consciousness.

"A Sacred Blooded's physical prowess greatly improves. And the stronger the love they have for them, the stronger their power. The blood awakens the instinct to protect their loved ones."

"Oh yeah, now I remember something like that..."

But he never expected there would be much use for that power in real life. Mostly because people rarely found themselves needing to kill one another in peacetime.

This also meant there were very few who'd seen the effects in reality. What would happen to her once she'd ingested so much blood?

"What do you think of me, Ryouta? It captures the heart of my minion, does it not?"

When he saw her, his first honest thought was:

What's going on? She's beautiful, but not in a human way...

She hadn't transformed into a curvy woman; her tattered dress hadn't mended itself. But her eyes were such a bright red that he could clearly see them, even by the light of the moon alone.

And it was hard to put it into words exactly, but they were so alluring that it made him uncomfortable.

It was almost as if internally, Shiren had completely transformed into something else.

Wow, there's no question that you are the most beautiful girl in the world right now. Honestly, even more than Ouka.

"You're pretty, but your eyes are *really* bloodshot."

"Lay off. Now, I think it's time to return to the battlefield."

"Do I bore you so much that you insist on licking blood? Die!" Sasara slashed downward.

And Shiren sent her, along with her sword, flying in the air. With barely a swipe.

"What...? Why am I...?" Sasara also seemed unable to process the situation.

"Death will be your penance for the crime of harming my minion."

The way she was speaking, the sentence sounded less like a personal declaration and more like an inescapable truth.

Right after that, two fissures ran parallel up and down Shiren's back, and two appendages that looked like wings slowly unfurled.

When the wings fully showed themselves, they spread as if they had a will of their own.

They were large and black, and they would probably go well with a high-slit dress.

"Hey, those look like they're from a fallen angel or Dracula or something, don't they...?"

But he didn't feel dread as he would from a monster.

Instead, it was more of an utter nobility, one that was found only among the gods.

"Ahhh, now I understand all the reasons why you acted so high and mighty..."

Obviously, all the people of the world would look like trash next to her if this was what she really was.

"Well, I believe regular Sacred Blooded probably atrophied a long time ago. We were not persecuted by humans simply because we drank blood. It is because our true form is so monstrous that they tried to erase us. But our family is still able to use this power properly, and that is exactly why we were made into the Imperial family, and why we carry the name Sarano."

"No... Is this not the Goddess of Blood...?" Sasara murmured, and Ryouta recalled the religious statue of a deity he'd seen at the cathedral.

Shiren was the spitting image.

"How unfair... I am an Imperial guard! And yet, just looking at her, I...I cannot take a step!"

Sasara was bewildered. No—she was beyond bewildered. Tears were gathering in her eyes.

A skilled swordswoman could tell the strength of an opponent at a glance, but it was impossible to imagine a power that would drive her to tears in the midst of battle.

That meant this wasn't even a battle anymore.

"Now, shall we continue? Harming my minion...harming Ryouta...will cost you a great deal." Shiren slowly made her way toward Sasara. The whole thing had already come to an end.

She lightly knocked away Sasara's sword. In the next moment, Shiren punched her so hard, she went flying.

Before she even had the chance to stand up, Shiren knocked her into the air again. It was like a lion playing with a rabbit.

Wait, this was no time for him to stare!

"Shiren, calm down. If you don't..."

She'll die.

In just another minute, Sasara could very well be turned into a mangled corpse as he watched. Shiren couldn't afford to have new crimes weighing on her shoulders right when her old ones were about to be forgiven.

"Shiren, listen to me... Stop!"

It wasn't working. His tattered body wasn't letting him scream. Even if he could, he wasn't positive she could hear him.

Then his only choice was to stop her by standing in front of her.

She was a hundred times scarier than Sasara, but what else could he do? Stopping his master was part of his service to her.

He rose like a zombie. His whole body coursed with unbelievable pain; he almost felt as though he could learn to find a new kind of pleasure from it.

And then Ryouta Fuyukura ran. His legs felt like they would shatter with his first step, his innards felt like they would explode with his second step, and he felt like his third would take him straight down into the after-life, but still, he ran. For his master—he could never do such a thing for himself. He had already abandoned himself, and that's why he could do it.

"Shiren, stop!"

He wasn't sure if he got between them while stumbling forward, or if he stumbled forward while getting between them.

As Shiren was about to deliver the final blow, he embraced her.

The color of Shiren's eyes returned to normal, as if the contact between them had flipped some kind of switch.

"Huh? Ryouta, what was I…?"

"I… I did it…"

But that didn't mean this was going to end without any casualties. Sasara's breath was coming in faint gasps. Without proper care, she would die.

He supported her in his arms.

"Hey, don't die on us. You won't be able to protect the Emperor anymore!"

"How…good-natured must you be? I… I played you foul…"

"I'm not doing this for you! You wouldn't want your master to be a murderer, either, would you?! If someone was on the brink of death because of a mistake Ouka made, then you'd try to save them with everything you could, right? Neither of us could bear seeing our master carry that sin for the rest of her life!"

"Oh…"

He figured he could find some common ground in their status as minions, and it looked like it was working.

"And you still want to stay by your master's side, don't you?"

"Yes, no matter how many times I am reborn, forever…"

Then there was only one option here.

"Hey, Shiren, does blood have nutrients in it?"

"Yes. That's why humans can also recover when they receive a blood donation—blood is just a bundle of nutrients."

"Okay. Sasara, lick some off my right arm. I bled enough to almost kill me thanks to you, so you can probably get a good mouthful in."

"I—I could never fathom drinking a man's blood..."

Sasara's face suddenly went red as blood in embarrassment.

Wait, come on, this isn't the time to be embarrassed about anything!

"You use blood in cooking, don't you? It's the same thing!"

"Ugh... But..."

"Would you rather die?!"

"Very well..." Hesitantly, Sasara slowly began licking away at his blood. The entire time, she acted like it was the most mortifying thing in the world. "Urgh... I can't believe...I have to...do this..."

Sasara ran her tongue along his arm with obvious anguish.

"You will never say anything of this to anyone... If word gets out that I licked the blood of a man, I will kill you, and then I will die."

"Wait, is this really that embarrassing to a Sacred Blooded...?"

"Of course. It's almost on the same level as getting naked in front of someone..."

"Whaaaaaat?! I didn't know that!"

Sasara gripped Ryouta hard, apparently trying to force him closer to her. "And now because I've told you...see...you will have to take responsibility... If you don't, you will sully the distinguished Tatsunami family name..."

"Responsibility? How?"

"Of course, the one I love is Her Imperial Majesty, but you know society isn't very accepting of love between women, right...? So, for example, when the time comes, you will f...fake marry me."

This was going in an odd direction.

"I finally understand why I kept finding you about to get your blood sucked, Ryouta."

He heard a grim voice coming from behind him.

"You've tricked so many people like this! This is all you ever did in Japan, and when it turned into a slaughterhouse, you ran away! I knew it!"

"What are you talking about?! That's not it at all! I didn't trick anybody!"

"I don't want to hear your excuses! And get away from that guard right this instant! You are my minion, Ryouta! You are to be serving me! I will sue you!"

At least sue me for a more serious offense... Ryouta, exhausted, sprawled out on the grass. "*Sigh*, I'd love to have some liver to eat right now."

"Let's head to a barbecue place after this. But we'll have to stop the bleeding first; otherwise they won't let you in. But even if the guard cleared everybody out, no one's coming yet. There's a problem with this security system."

Sasara didn't seem to have any energy to think about her next steps, either, and she was staring up at the sky.

"I can't believe...I ended up drinking so much of a man's blood... That was my first time... Oh, Father, Mother, I have been sullied..."

It sounded as if he'd done something very wrong, but it was too late now.

Now what should they do? It was obvious there had been a commotion here; there was no getting around it.

And Kiyomizu was murmuring in her sleep, "Oh, most noble Ryouta. Please put the kitty ears on next. Hee-hee-heh-heh-heh..."

"I'm scared; I can't wake her up, but she'll be executed if we just leave her here and they find out who she is..."

"It'll be fine, don't you think?" Shiren retorted. "She's still Japanese; we can't kill her. Actually, if we carry out any executions, since Japan doesn't recognize the Empire as sovereign, that would cause some huge problems."

"Then I guess we'll head home quietly," Ryouta suggested. "It'd be bad if they found out about Sasara's involvement."

"Truly, what a bind," said a third voice. "I almost want you to be the Emperor instead."

"Yeah— Gah!! Ouka?!"

Ouka was standing right beside them. Sasara's face was so pale, it was almost blue.

"Oh, hi there! That was a marvelous action play." Alfoncina XIII stood beside her, too.

"When did you get here, Ouka?"

"This is my castle. I can appear whenever I want. To tell the truth, I saw everything. I was thinking about jumping in if things got too bad."

"In my opinion, things *did* get pretty bad, but...it's a miracle no one died. Wait—you knew about all this?!"

"I received word from the fourteen other Imperial guards of Sasara's treason."

"*All* her coworkers ratted her out?! And wait, why is the archbishop here?"

"Kimura heard you were just ever so slightly a minion, so she was here to ask me questions."

"Who's Kimura?"

"It's Alfoncina's real name, remember? Matsuko Kimura."

Now he remembered.

"Hold on! I thought I told you never to use my real name! What about my dignity?!" Alfoncina seemed rather flustered.

"Dignity? Not when you sound panicked like that. Oh, and she's here for a photoshoot."

"A photoshoot?" That wasn't a word he was expecting, so Ryouta repeated it for clarification.

"I'm the one selling Alfoncina as an idol. We have a photo collection going on sale next month. We have all the publishing rights, and if we calculate the number of members in her fan club, then I believe we'll make gross profits in the ballpark of ten billion. It is the perfect way of acquiring foreign currency."

"Ten billion? How many fans do you have?!"

"How about you, Ryouta, dear? Do you want a copy?"

"I'll take two."

Shiren slapped him from behind.

"Now then, the typical true ending would be Sasara getting executed for treason. I do love blood and gore, but if that goes public, then the name of the Imperial Guard would be marred, which would also be embarrassing for me, so I'll let it pass this time."

"You like blood and gore?!"

Sasara immediately began groveling. "Thank you, Your Imperial Majesty!" This was definitely the right thing for her to do in this situation. "Um, could receiving such compassion from you, Your Imperial Majesty, mean you feel at least the slightest bit of attraction toward me?"

Or maybe she hadn't done any self-examining at all.

"I won't make this incident public, but you did make a mess of my garden, so I'm docking the next year from your salary."

Ouka completely ignored the troublesome question. He was a total outsider, but Ryouta sympathized. Being the Emperor must be a tough job.

"Now we will finally get to the topic at hand. Shiren, Ryouta?"

Shiren's shoulders tensed when her name was called.

"Honestly, what sort of relationship do you two have? What do you want to do? I'll get mad, so be honest!"

"You will?!" Didn't you usually say *I won't get mad*?

"Of course," replied Ouka. "I was taught to always express how I feel honestly. Think about it—how annoying would it be if all I ever said was *I-it's not like I like fried potatoes or anything!* despite liking fried potatoes very much?"

"Why *that* example?!"

"Say it anyway. Since I'm human, too, it is not entirely impossible that I might want to grant wishes like Shenlong does. At least once every million requests."

"So a zero percent chance, basically!"

"And now, Shiren, I believe you understand the significance of the awakening you went through not too long ago, right?" Ouka turned to Shiren.

She was just looking at her, but that alone was overwhelming enough. There was literal power in her eyes.

"Um…uh…I'm sorry, Your Majesty…" Shiren's head drooped, like a child being discovered pulling pranks.

This wasn't a sisterly relationship at all.

"Well, Shiren? What do you want to do? Say it."

"I… Um…"

She couldn't speak. If she did, it would be treason against the Emperor. Not only that, but it would also betray Ryouta. Ouka was Ryouta's first love, after all.

"Beeeeep. Time's up. You'll never get a job if you interview like that. Then let me ask someone else. What is it you want to do, Ryouta?"

Ouka turned to look at Ryouta, a faint smile on her face with depths unknown behind it.

That was the kind of girl Ouka had been, ever since elementary school—and that was why he had to do everything he could; otherwise he would be no match for her.

"Say something that will make me *hmm*. Only then will I think it over." Ouka crossed her arms and chuckled.

But Ryouta had been ready for this long before they even came here.

He knelt on one knee. "Your Imperial Majesty, my master has no friends!!!!!" he cried, in the loudest voice he could muster with his battered body. "If I may speak frankly, one reason is that my master... Gah, forget it! One reason is because she's so high and mighty about everything! I was really frustrated with her at the beginning, too!"

"Come on, why are you insulting me now?! Shut up, Ryouta!"

He ignored Shiren's complaint, of course. "But ninety percent of her loneliness is because she's a felon, and because of her bloodline—she's the daughter of the previous emperor, and the current one's little sister. And so that's why she and her classmates have put distance between them! They just want to chat—they just want to be friends, but they feel like they have to stay away!"

Ryouta inhaled deeply.

"And she takes really good care of her minions, too. Please let me speak as a minion; there are very few masters as excellent as she is. That is why, as her minion, I want my master to make friends without anything holding her back. I want her to be even happier, to smile more."

No one said anything to interrupt him.

"But you decided you would take down all the walls in her way, Your Imperial Majesty. So please allow me to look after her. Please wait for her to make friends, just for a little while until she doesn't need me anymore."

Shiren silently stared at Ryouta, surprise all over her face.

"And there is one person I want Shiren to be friends with over anyone else."

"Who?"

"You, Your Imperial Majesty."

Both Shiren and Ouka simultaneously looked at him in surprise.

"Shiren has always wanted to amend relations with her older sister, the Emperor. She almost calls you *Big Sis* sometimes. You wouldn't want to miss this chance to get close enough that you could talk openly with her, either, would you, Your Majesty? If I cannot ensure my master's dreams can come true, then I doubt I'll be able to find another—"

"Enough. I understand."

Ryouta bowed reverently. His body was still throbbing, but he endured.

He still had to behave properly before the Emperor as Shiren's servant.

He lifted his head slightly to look at Ouka. She appeared to be saying, *How impudent of you.*

With his head still raised, he took a glance at Shiren.

Her face said she wanted to run from there. He knew how she felt. He'd feel exactly the same if he were in her place. This was much worse than just waiting for the results of an interview or test.

"I see. I hear your opinion. But I still have the right to make the final decision."

"Yes, I understand that, Your Imperial Majesty."

"Please stop using polite language with me. It's making me sick. Now, Shiren."

Ouka slowly placed herself right in front of Shiren, then heavily rested both of her hands on Shiren's shoulders.

"Do you realize what you're doing warrants an apology to me?"

"Oh, yes... Your Imperial Majesty, I'm sorry...," Shiren murmured, her voice barely above a whisper.

"This only makes me angry."

"I know..."

"However"—Ouka gently embraced Shiren—"I still know I haven't been able to love you as my little sister for a long time." She lightly kissed Shiren on the cheek. "Forgive me. As my apology, we'll forget about this whole thing. Ryouta is your minion. You should live together."

"Wha...?"

"Did you not hear me? I'll repeat myself. Ryouta is your minion, so you should live together!"

"Thank you so much, Your Imperial Majesty!" Shiren returned the hug in spite of herself.

"And don't call me that anymore. I am the only person in this world you can call a sister, so what's the point if you call me otherwise?"

"Okay...Big Sis."

The moment had finally come. Shiren could stand before Ouka and officially refer to her as sister.

"It sounds a little forced after such a dramatic pause, but sure." When Ouka let Shiren go, she put her hands on her hips with a sigh. "Now, you two work hard, okay? And let me just give you a piece of advice, because people's hearts are ever changing. There will be plenty of times when you'll find your heart set on someone else, Ryouta. And don't forget I am a top-notch politician who created an independent nation from within a developed country."

Once she went briskly over everything she wanted to say, she went back into the castle.

"Bye now," she called. "You'll be moving tomorrow."

"Please wait, my Imperial Majesty!" Sasara shouted, following after her.

"Awww, I wonder which part of that was an honest expression of emotion?" mused Alfoncina. "Anyway, I have several political talks with Her Majesty to go over, so I'm going back to the castle. Good-bye, my dears." With that, she followed them in as well.

"...Good-bye, Kimura."

"Don't call me Kimura!"

And then only Ryouta and Shiren were left.

"Then I guess we go home now, Shiren."

"Yeah. We'll go straight home. I have a lot to say about how you view me as a lonely person with no friends."

"I mean, it's true. How else was I supposed to put it? Ouch..."

When he started walking, it just reminded him how much his entire body hurt. It was a relief his arm had stopped bleeding, though—Sacred Blooded saliva must have a strong coagulating agent in it.

"I know. But it still put me in a tough spot. I'm going to start working hard to make a hundred friends right away."

"Yeah, do it."

"And I have to say this now, while I can." Shiren slipped out of Ryouta's field of vision.

"If you want to say something, at least say it to my face."

"How insensitive. I'm just embarrassed."

"I went to school in a collar and the girls' uniform. Nothing scares me."

He could tell Shiren was behind him right then.

"Oh, I'm not going to kick you in the back of your knee or prank you in other ways."

"You don't have to explain. What is it, then?"

"Thank you." Shiren wrapped her arms around him from behind.

Both their bodies were beaten and battered, but that only meant each person's warmth was more directly connected to the other's.

This was the greatest honor a minion could receive after saving his master.

"I dunno, I feel like you have some ulterior motive, and that scares me... I don't mind getting some thanks, though. Well, good luck making friends..."

"And I need to work hard to make sure my big sis doesn't take Ryouta away from me... *(whisper, whisper)*"

"Hmm? Did you say something?"

"You're imagining things. Don't worry about it. And when we get home, I'm putting the collar on."

"Awww, the collar again? But I guess I am a minion."

Also, in case you were wondering, Kiyomizu reportedly woke up early the next morning at five.

©Hiroki Ozaki

EPILOGUE

"Argh… Everything hurts…"

"You can do it. I'm in a lot of pain myself…"

Ryouta and Shiren came to school wrapped in bandages. Their new home was also next to the castle, so it took them longer to get to school.

Even though they had fallen straight to sleep from exhaustion, the movers had come at six in the morning and woken them up to take their things to the castle. They had been somewhat excited to start a life of luxury, but once they got there, they found that a house that looked exactly like their old one had been built beside the castle. It just barely fit within the grounds.

To Ryouta, this felt like Ouka-style spite.

But they were glad they'd borne the pain and come to school anyway.

"Oh, Fuyukura—I mean, Sarano, congrats."

"Hey, c'mon, you gotta be polite to the Emperor's sister!"

"But isn't it just weirder if we put her on a pedestal?"

"Morning, Shiren!"

There were a lot more students openly greeting Shiren—maybe word had already gotten out to some that the Emperor had made amends with her sister.

It seemed her friendless situation would be solved a lot quicker than Ryouta thought.

When they entered the classroom, Tamaki was there, too.

"I'm so happy for you two. What are the bandages about, though? Don't tell me…you two were planning on burning yourselves alive…? I'm sorry; I can't believe I crossed the line and talked about your past…"

"My past isn't that dark, so don't worry about it."

"I do worry. The only person whose blood I know the taste of in this class is Ryouta." After that strange admission, Tamaki hurriedly turned to look away.

That on its own was okay, but for some reason, Shiren stomped on his foot.

"Don't worry about it. I just got a sudden urge to step on you," she said. That didn't make any sense, but neither did she sometimes.

The atmosphere at school was different from usual, but the school bell rang when it was time, and the homeroom teacher entered the class.

"Erm, we have a transfer student today."

When he heard that, Ryouta got an awful sinking feeling in his stomach.

And he was right on the money.

"It's lovely to meet you all. I am Kiyomizu Jouryuuji. I am Sacred Blooded. And I am the wonderful Ryouta's lover!" Kiyomizu calmly strode into the classroom.

"Hold on! No way, *no way* this is happening!"

"I will always be by your side, even if I have to take on a false persona. It's all right. I won't hurt any of your classmates."

"You just said you have a false persona!! At least keep *that* much under wraps!"

"What else can I say? The only truth in this world is my love for you, Ryouta, my dearest. Oh, that was a wonderful thing to say, if I do say so myself!"

"There's nothing wonderful about it! You can't just decide it is and tell everyone!"

"Awww, I'm sure we all want to coo over Jouryuuji's words of love, but keep that on hold a moment. We have more transfer students."

The teacher was not very good at finding a segue.

"Well, come in...new students."

The two who came into the classroom were none other than Ouka and Sasara Tatsunami.

"Greetings, subjects. I am your emperor. Kneel before me. Lick my boots. Oh, and you, sitting next to Ryouta, get up out of your seat."

"Hello, everyone, my name is Sasara Tatsunami. Please remember that any slight toward Her Imperial Majesty will result in your erasure."

Nobody had ever introduced themselves this way. Ever.

"Oh, I believe I just saw that boy over there making eyes at the Emperor—you're expelled."

"Hey, come on, you two, give it a rest! You can't just do that!" Ryouta, of course, couldn't help but comment.

"What? We used to be classmates, Ryouta, so joining you in school shouldn't be a problem at all. You narrow-minded boy."

"Now that the Emperor is coming to school, I must accompany her as her Imperial guard. It is not for you! It is definitely not for you!"

"I know. You don't have to emphasize it like that…" Ryouta was certain this arrangement would bring nothing but trouble.

"Good luck, Shiren. Let's make this a fair fight." Ouka gave Shiren a suggestive smile.

"That's just what I was hoping for, Big Sis!"

That was the first time he saw Shiren so defiant.

Ryouta, alone in the uproarious classroom, thought to himself—*Maybe I should go back to Japan.*

AFTERWORD

Hello, I am Kisetsu Morita. Some readers of GA Bunko might be thinking, *Who the heck is this guy?* but I am a small-time light novel author. I hope you'll keep an eye out for me in the future.

This novel was based on my own real experiences. In high school, when I climbed up a mountain, I found myself in a secret village filled with beautiful girls. I was trapped there once a resident found me, and so I lived there for two and a half years... Okay, you got me; obviously, I have never been so fortunate. I mean, if I found a place like that, I wouldn't leave after just two and a half years.

This time on *You Call That Service?*, I decided not to settle on a set number of characters and instead concentrate on creating characters I would like to see. And so I think you'll very obviously see what the author is into. I also wrote about a country and city I personally would like to live in. Aw man, I wish there was a hidden village full of beautiful girls somewhere out there...

And as usual (but for my first time in GA Bunko, though), my acknowledgements. Thank you to my editor, S. This story was born because S-san treated me to food. I was told I had to write about it. Oh, it seems someone else is here.

Many of my biggest thanks to the illustrator, Hiroki Ozaki. I never imagined the concept art I would get for this. I could even say that S-san and Ozaki-san transformed this work from vague Morita ideas into a defined shape.

I'm sure this is true for any book, but this one has an especially strong influence from the editor and illustrator. I hope the both of you will continue to help me in the volumes to come!

And lastly, to all of you who read this book: Thank you. As an appendix, I will include a spell on the next line that will bring happiness:

You call that service? You call that service?

If you chant this incantation ten times in one day, then you will become a popular head-turner. It is especially effective if you say it in front of the person you have a crush on. Don't worry about feeling embarrassed; please pretend it's like a silly punishment game and give it a try. It's also like an advertisement for the book, and that makes the author happy.

Well then, I hope to see you next time.

■ Question for Shiren
What's the key to staying healthy?

Tomatoes.

You definitely just
made that up.

■ Question for Tamaki
What is your favorite book?

HARDCOVERS...
THEY MAKE EXCELLENT WEAPONS.

It's what's inside
that counts!

■ Question for Kiyomizu
What is is a very philosophical element to
Ryouta's name. As you know, in Japanese, a single
nd can have many meanings, and *ryou* can mean "to end"
nded." However, in the second part of his name, we encounter th
ta, which can be construed as an explosive sounding *Ta!* Like th
. So if we put these two together, I believe Ryouta's name signi
ending of all things and then the beginning of all things. T
tially means Ryouta is, without a doubt, a god. A
urse, my love for God is undui

At least listen to
the question first.

■ Question for Alfoncina
I told her I liked her, but she turned me down.
What was the problem?

Because you were carrying
a body pillow of a cute girl.

Where did that come from?!

■ Question for Sasara
What is it you like about the Empress?

Her divine beauty.
Her face. Her body. Her big eyes. The yawns
she stifles. The sigh she makes when she sees a stack of
paperwork. Her dignity as a ruler. Her fashion sense.
Her love for her country. The kindness she shows
once a month.

She's kind to you
only once a month...?

■ Question for Ouka
Our family budget has been very tight,
and we are unable to pay taxes. What
should we do, Your Imperial Majesty?

Work more.

Can't you be a little more
considerate of your people...?